WIFE OF A MISFIT

A *CAMERON* SPIN-OFF

JADE JONES

www.jadedpublications.com

TO BE NOTIFIED OF NEW RELEASES,
CONTESTS, GIVEAWAYS,

AND BOOK SIGNINGS IN YOUR AREA, TEXT
BOOKS TO **25827**

This novel is a work of fiction. Any reference to real people, events, establishments, or locales is intended only to give the fiction a sense of reality and authenticity. Other names, characters, and incidents occurring in the work are either the product of the author's imagination or are used fictitiously, as are those fictionalized events and events that involve real persons. Any character that happens to share the name of a person who is any acquaintance of the author, past or present, is purely coincidental and is in no way intended to be an actual account involving that person.

NOTE FROM THE AUTHOR

The following characters are from *"Cameron 7."* In order to enhance your reading experience, I would highly recommend reading the *"Cameron"* series!

WARNING: *This story is not for the faint-hearted...*

PROLOGUE

Standing on the edge of the CNN building in downtown Atlanta, I thought about all of the wasted years I'd spent on a man who had never loved me. I felt so foolish, so motherfucking naïve.

How could I have allowed that sorry ass nigga to treat me this way for so long?

The question burned in my brain as I contemplated suicide. Every time that I blinked, I envisioned how my funeral would play out; the people who would attend, the fake ass tears that would be shed. Sad to say, I never imagined things would one day lead to this.

Gentle cricket noises could be heard in the distance, coupled with the sounds of impatient drivers beeping their horns. The full moon illuminated the dark, starry skies stretching overhead.

As my toes hung over the ledge, a strong gust of wind blew through my hair and an uneasy chill sat on my heart. I was barefoot in nothing but a Chanel cocktail dress and smeared makeup. A night of nonstop drinking and heavy drugs had me not giving a fuck about my appearance lately—which was totally unlike me. Normally, I was always on my shit, but because of him, I was now at an all-time low.

I can't believe I'm really at this point...

Blinded by emotions, I was too upset to realize that what I was preparing to do was the dumbest thing ever. Contrary to popular belief, I had always been a smart girl, with a fair amount of rationality and good judgment. But the day that I fell in love with him—the day that I gave my heart to that selfish, trifling ass bitch, all my common sense pretty much went out the window. For years, I had played the fool for a nigga who had been playing me the whole time.

I had done everything under the sun to prove my loyalty to a man that didn't even respect me. I'd sold my body for him, I'd lied for him, hell I'd even killed for him. I had literally sacrificed everything and everyone I knew and loved for him. I'd given him my all and in return he gave me shit.

God, I feel so fucking stupid...

Warm tears cascaded down my cheeks as I took a small step forward. I shivered a bit at the rush of cool air that greeted me. The heels of my feet were now the only things keeping me grounded. One more inch and it'd all be over...

When I looked down, I saw heavy traffic and walking pedestrians who were completely oblivious to the woman above them preparing to jump. I had never been so close to death.

To tell the truth, in that moment, I felt free. Like the chains around my wrists and ankles had finally been unshackled. *If this is what*

*I have to do to make the pain go away, then fuck
it...* To me, it was worth it.

A crooked grin lingered in the corner of
my lips. It was the first time I had smiled in ages,
and for once, I felt like I was the one in control of
my destiny. Like the weight of my burdens had
finally been lifted. Closing my eyes, I prayed for
atonement before leaping off the edge of the
building...

1
DIANA

How did I get here?

Every day that I opened my eyes and every night before I fell asleep, I asked myself that same mind-bending question over and over again.

How in the hell did I get here?

There was once a time when I was on top of the world, living life to the fullest with no worries in sight, but unfortunately that time had ended. The day that I was arrested was the day that my life pretty much ended. My power, freedom and independence had been stripped away, leaving me naked and vulnerable with nothing but an inmate number to call my own.

Instead of the posh condos I'd grown accustomed to living in, I was now forced to call this shitty, minimum security prison home. And unlike life outside of prison, there was no coming and going as I pleased. No doing whatever I wanted. Those privileges had been revoked the day that I was convicted.

Speaking of my conviction, I nearly fainted when the verdict came back that I was guilty. The jury showed no mercy because of the magnitude of my crimes—especially since a child was involved. Sex trafficking and exploiting and promoting sex with a minor was what I'd been charged with.

I would never forget the disgusted look in the judge's eyes when he sentenced me. I barely even heard the condescending speech he gave afterwards because I was in such a state of shock and disbelief.

Fucking around with my ex had landed me in a world of trouble. Thirty years' worth of trouble to be exact. Tariq Haddad a.k.a. Rico was a pimp, strip club owner, and business man from upstate New York that had me at hello. To be honest, I fell for him hard and I fell for him fast. So fast that I had no time to realize he wasn't the answer to my problems.

He had me sprung like an old box mattress; so gone, that I didn't want to return. I'd always had a foolish desire to love the wrong men.

From the beginning, I knew about his complex career, but I still allowed him to drag me into his chaotic world...and to keep it real, I loved every single moment of it. Rico had me wrapped around all ten of his fingers, and I was down to do whatever—which included getting involved in something I knew wasn't legal or morally sound.

I was well aware of the repercussions, but I still rolled with the punches. The revenue was good, the nigga I was making it with was amazing, and the dick, incomparable. Like a fool, I held him down to my own detriment.

I was just that head over heels for him. Before him there wasn't anyone who had that much control over me. Rico owned my mind, body, and soul. He showed me what it was like to be with a real nigga, and introduced me to a way of life that I wasn't at all used to prior to meeting him.

We were making so much money together, pulling in at least fifty grand a month. We had more funds than we knew what to do with. Everything was going great until the police raided our mansion and arrested me on the spot for running a human sex trafficking ring. And to make matters worse, every girl who worked for him testified to the allegations in court.

Each and every single one of them got up on that stand and lied, tossing my ass under the bus just to save their precious procurer. Never in a million years did I think my own girls would set me up and turn against me...Obviously, I didn't know how the game worked.

After my conviction, I was shipped to the Indiana Women's Prison in Indianapolis, which only housed the mentally ill, pregnant, and older inmates. The only reason they sent me there was because at the time of my arrest, I'd found out that I was three weeks pregnant. Unfortunately, I ended up losing the baby before reaching a full month. Stress and the fact that I was going through this shit alone had caused me to miscarry.

I spent a total of six months there before I was transferred to the Shulon Women's Correctional Facility in Gainesville, Georgia. It was a lot stricter than Indiana and way less lenient.

Being locked up was tough. No one wrote me, no one came to visit me, and no one was there to comfort me during my incarceration. Everyone that I knew had abandoned me, including so-called friends. Because of a lack of support, life was lonely and depressing.

Although I tried very hard to keep my spirits up most days I just felt like dying. There were even times when I thought about putting myself out of my misery—but I didn't have the balls to. Instead, I chose to serve my bid and make the best of my situation. Thankfully, I had a cool ass celly that helped to keep my mind off the bullshit.

"B, why the hell you caking all that shit under ya eyes?" I asked her. It wasn't until now that I noticed Nyri playing makeup in the foggy ass mirror above our toilet. How we both managed to co-inhabit a tiny 6x8 room was still a mystery to me.

Nyri was here for aggravated robbery, kidnapping, and first degree battery. She was a cute, Puerto-Rican chick who looked nothing like she was capable of committing the crimes she was charged with. Her baby doll face, soft brown eyes, and piercing dimples made her look as innocent as a church girl on Sunday. Too bad she wasn't.

"*Dios mio!* Bitch, you ain't heard?! Mr. Asante's coming back to work today and I need to look good for when he sees me." Her voice was a thrilling whisper and I read excitement all in her expression.

I hadn't seen her look this happy in ages and I really didn't understand why. No one ever came to see her during visitation, so I couldn't figure out who on Earth she was talking about.

"Who the hell is Mr. Asante?" With a confused expression, I watched as she piled on a thick layer of eyeliner. You would've thought she was prepping for a conjugal visit or some shit.

Obviously, we couldn't have real products because of prison regulations. However, inmates were creative when it came to fabricating their own makeup goods, brushes and utensils. Like my roommate for example. This bitch could make eyeliner, lipstick, and blush by using nothing but candy, crayons and colored pencils. I swear this hoe deserved a bachelor's degree in arts and crafts.

Nyri's eyes lit up with amusement as she answered. "Oh, shit. I forgot, he left before you were even transferred here. That's why you don't know who he is," she explained.

"So you drawing all over ya face for a fucking prison guard? Am I hearing you right?"

"A prison guard that *might* one day be desperate enough to fuck me—"

"I doubt it," I laughed.

"Whatever. A girl can still fantasize," she said. "Anyway, he injured himself while coaching and had been on leave for like six months. That's why you've never seen him."

"Did I just hear someone say they don't know who Mr. Asante is?!" Bianca poked her triangular head in the room as if we'd personally invited her into our conversation. Since it was rec, all of the inmates in our pod were permitted to roam around freely. "Bitch, you *schleeeeeep*! How the fuck you don't know who Mr. Asante is?" Bianca said, inviting herself inside.

I swear the bitch was forever butting into someone else's business. She deserved a motherfucking award for being eavesdropper of the year. Aside from her nosiness, Bianca was a pretty, dark skinned girl who always wore her hair in bantu knots. Slim and tall in build, she reminded me of a fashion model for one of those popular, designer clothing lines.

"Girl, he's only the sexiest mothafucka they got working up in this bitch! The man so damn fine he looks like Jesus himself blessed his face! Wait until you see him, Diana! I'm telling you ya clit gon start twitching!"

Hearing her say that crazy ass shit made me burst out laughing. "Girl, bye. The only thing that could make my clit twitch is the judge telling me that I'm free. I'd probably suck his dick right on the spot."

Nyri joined us in laughter and I quickly remembered that I had a bone to pick with her. "Bitch, you over here giggling and shit but you the only fucking joke I see right now."

"How so?" she asked.

"Hoe, one minute you like dykes, the next minute you like dicks. You can't make up ya mothafucking mind for shit." Just last month, she had a girl and now she was painting her face for a nigga who wouldn't even look twice in our direction. "I swear you change teams more than LeBron!"

She laughed because she knew that it was true. "Fuck you, Dirty Diana!"

We were all laughing and having a good old time until someone called out "Count time ladies!"

Nyri and Bianca quickly scrambled out of the cell, but because I was on the top bunk it took me a bit longer to get my bearings.

From time to time, correctional officers performed routine counts to make sure that none of the prisoners were missing or somewhere they weren't supposed to be. It was annoying as hell, but I wasn't exactly in the position to argue against policies.

As soon as I climbed out of the bed, I fixed my clothes and started for the door—but stopped suddenly when I saw a tall, cinnamon colored man standing there with his arms folded. There was a disapproving look on his perfectly chiseled face that showed he wasn't too pleased with me taking my sweet time. Nothing about him seemed welcoming...but lawd was he fine!

My eyes briefly scanned the nametag on his shirt that read K. Asante.

Damn...So this is the nigga that got all these hoes' pussies wet.

The man was panty-drenchingly rugged as fuck. His sheer physicality gave him power. He had to be at least 6"3 and was built like an NFL player. The uniform he wore hugged his broad chest and made his biceps look massive. His muscular body proclaimed his general fitness to the world, and I wouldn't have been surprised if he hit the gym every single day. In addition to his buff body, he had a low cut fade, a neatly tapered beard, and thick, juicy lips that made me want to cum all over myself.

Needless to say, I was pleasantly surprised by his singular good looks. He was too damn fine to be working in some crusty ass prison.

I was completely lost in a trance until he quickly snapped me out of it. "Inmate, why are you in the cell still when everyone is *clearly* out of theirs? Did you not hear me call count? I wasn't aware that we had a prisoner with a hearing impairment."

I casually laughed him off. "My bad, dude. Relax. I was just—"

"When you speak to me, you address me as Mr. Asante," he interjected, his tone rough. "Hell, even a simple 'sir' will suffice." He spoke smooth, sternly, and with conviction. His voice was deep, powerful and somewhat intimidating. Because he was putting me on the spot, I deliberately avoided his intense eyes. "Look at me," he said in a commandingly calm tone.

Tearing my stare from the floor, I looked up to meet his gaze. His eyes were hazel with tiny specks of amber, and reminded me of leaves in the spring time. There were three faint scars on his face, two on either cheek and one between his brows but it didn't detract from his good looks in the slightest. Even while he was being uptight, it was hard not to find him abundantly attractive.

"In here, I'm not your dude," he clarified. "I'm not one of ya lil' buddies. And I sure as shit ain't ya friend...so spare me the damn excuses, aight. Next time you're in your cell when I call count, that's an automatic trip to the SHU. Do I make myself clear?"

The security housing unit, or SHU, was a place that I never wanted to visit. Inmates there were locked up in their cells for 23 hours a day and allowed only 3 showers a week. Rumor had it that some of them even went crazy after spending so much time in solitary confinement, away from general population. I didn't want those problems at all, so I tried to stay on my best behavior.

The entire pod was fraught with tension as all of the women waited for my response. Looking down in shame, I slowly nodded my head in surrender. The fact that everyone was now looking in my direction had me feeling uncharacteristically small. I hated him for embarrassing me in front of everyone. In the distance, Bianca smothered a laugh at my utter humiliation.

"I don't do head gestures," he said. There was unspoken criticism in the sharpness of his gaze. Mr. Asante wasn't very fond of me at all. That was beyond clear. "I asked you a question and I need a direct response," he said. "Otherwise, I'll feel like you don't comprehend. And trust me, I have *very* little tolerance for inmates who don't comprehend."

Normally, I was one to go tit for tat because I was petty like that. But behind bars, I couldn't challenge authority without dire consequences. As much as I hated to admit it, prison had broken me.

Instead of replying with some witty comeback, I nodded my head sheepishly. "I comprehend loud and clear, Mr. Asante..." I said, my tone somewhat hesitant. I felt like dying from pure mortification.

There was an unconvinced silence between us but he refused to further speak on the matter. With a look of cool distaste, he walked off, leaving me to feel like a child who'd just been reprimanded by their father.

Once Mr. Asante was out of earshot, Nyri leaned over and whispered in my ear. "Girl, you bet not try that nigga like that again. I should've warned you, he ain't the one."

Bianca quickly piped up in agreement. "Yeah, he may be easy on the eyes and all, but the nigga don't fuck around. If I were you, I'd tread really carefully."

I snorted in disgust, not feeling the way they unilaterally decided that I was in the wrong. The fact that he didn't fuck around was more than obvious to me. But in my opinion, all of the guards were just a bunch of overzealous assholes, always acting high strung when it came to their career. You could easily see how much they loved taking advantage of their authority.

As far as I was concerned, Mr. Asante was no different. From that moment on, I knew that I wouldn't like him. "Girl, please. Fuck him. I ain't worried about that nigga or his swollen ass ego."

I could already tell we weren't going to get along very well.

***

The following afternoon, Bianca, Nyri, and I decided to burn some energy by doing laps in the prison yard. Everyone else was either exercising or sitting around chit-chatting. Since we all were incarcerated there weren't many options offered to combat boredom.

As I looked around the yard, I couldn't believe that this was actually my life now. Living with a pack of ruthless killers, thieves, and carjackers all under one roof—and the most violent of them all was making her way over towards me.

Yuri Palmer had recently been released from the administrative segregation unit—which was a prison within a prison—and was now back in general population. As a matter of fact, I was the reason she had been sent there to begin with.

Yuri was a burly, bulldog looking butch that loved starting shit with me whenever the opportunity presented itself. She was also Tabitha's sister, who was the wife of the married man I used to fuck back in Cleveland.

Wayne and I had dated for months, despite me knowing about his marriage. Not only did he take care of me financially, he made me love him to the point where I no longer cared about his wife and kids. A woman's nightly companion shouldn't have been a married man, but I just couldn't leave him alone. We had no plans of ever ending our affair—until Tabitha confronted me one day in the parking lot of a busy mall.

She and I were arguing like a couple of fools when her 3-year-old son dropped his ball and ran off to retrieve it. Sadly, neither one of us noticed the Yukon Denali coming straight at him.

Yuri had a growing hatred for me because of her nephew's untimely murder. If her sister hadn't been so preoccupied with my nonsense, she would've never taken her eyes off of him. The incident was two years ago, but the wounds were still fresh.

If I could have, I would've gladly gone back in time to right my wrongs...but unfortunately, I couldn't. And Yuri had no intentions of forgetting what I'd done to her family and what I had taken from them. A child was killed and a union had been viciously torn apart...all because I couldn't respect someone else's marriage enough to keep my legs closed.

To be honest, I couldn't even be mad at Yuri for the way that she felt about me. Sometimes I hated myself for what I had caused. It was something that I had to live with for the rest of my life. And there wasn't a day that went by where that little boy didn't cross my mind. That fateful day would forever remain on my conscience...and every day that I spent behind bars I was paying for it.

When Yuri and I made eye contact, she glowered at me and then ran her index along her neck in a throat-slicing gesture. That bitch was gunning for me and she wouldn't stop until I was finally dead.

As soon as her girls noticed she was back in gen, they ran up to greet her with excitement. Yuri hung with nothing but tough looking studs who were known for Deebo-ing others. For the most part, they ran our pod and no one dared to get in their way. The last bitch who did was beaten so bad that she suffered a heart attack and died. Yuri and her girls were savages, and I knew it'd only be a matter of time before I was next.

"Fuck that bum bitch. Don't even worry about her. She ain't finna pop off," Nyri said. "She knows if she does, Mr. Asante will handle her. He ain't gon' let shit go down on his watch. He takes his job serious."

Glancing over in his direction, I scoffed, clearly disgusted by his grimness. "Yeah...so I've noticed." Sarcasm oozed from my tone as I watched him speak to a female officer who seemed a little too flirty and physical. Every so often, she would grab his arm and laugh.

Apparently, the inmates weren't the only ones excited about him coming back to work. I was perhaps the only one unenthused by his return. The way that he read me yesterday in front of everyone made our likelihood for harmony very slight.

When our gazes locked briefly, I felt tingly all over her. Something about his beautiful hazel eyes made me melt inside—but I quickly forgot that sensation in an instant after recalling how he'd checked me.

Quickly looking away, I prayed that he didn't think I was sweating him like all the other hoes. That most certainly wasn't the case.

"Girl, I know you ain't still salty about that lil' shit from yesterday," Nyri said, with a faint hint of laughter in her tone. "Look, he may've came off like a dick but he's good peoples for real. He just likes to act all tough. He's a good guy."

"*Good guy?*" I repeated, with heavy doubt in my voice.

"Yeah, Mr. Asante's cool as fuck. I mean, he coaches high school football. He donates regularly, and he's the only person who truly cares about the issues us inmates are faced with on a daily basis," Bianca pointed out.

I looked unsurprised by the news. The perfect picture they painted of him still wasn't enough to impress me.

She then went on to explain how he was always going to bat for the inmates at all of the board meetings and how he fought for proper but fair treatment. She also said that he was one of the few staff members who weren't corrupt or abusing the system for their own personal benefit.

"He may like to act all hard as a way to assert his position but he's cool peoples."

"*Hmph.* I sure as hell can't tell."

"Then try to stay on his good side," Bianca said before pinching my ass and running off.

I tried to hit her shoulder but her lanky ass moved with the quickness and precision of a fly avoiding being swatted. Since there was nothing else to do in prison but work out and goof off, I chased after her. I'd almost caught up with her too before a basketball came sailing towards me. I damn near tripped and broke my neck in an attempt to duck.

Of course, Yuri and her minions found the whole thing hilarious.

"Who the fuck threw this mothafucking ball?! 'Cuz obviously somebody want they mothafucking ass kicked!" Picking it up, I prepared to launch it right back at whoever had thrown it.

"Bitch, I gotta whole 'lotta ass! Come over here and get some!" Yuri said, walking rather tentatively towards me. She showed a complete lack of refinement despite weekly anger management classes. Her eyes were dancing with excitement as she glared at me. She was ready and willing to go blow for blow—and word was, she didn't fight fair.

Yuri's faithful goons were right at her side, ready to brawl, but I didn't give a fuck as I stepped forward too. We may've had our differences, and I felt terrible for what happened to her nephew, but I wasn't about to let any fucking body chump me off.

Nyri and Bianca quickly ran to my side as well, yet judging from their expressions I could tell they weren't looking to get hurt. *I don't know why I ever befriended these scary ass bitches*, I thought to myself.

Wrenching her hair back from her scalp, Nyri cast a rather desperate glance at the C.O.s in hopes that they would pick up on the tension. Unfortunately, they didn't notice because they were too busy talking amongst themselves.

Me and my girls were easily outnumbered and if a fight broke out things definitely wouldn't end in our favor but I didn't care. All that mattered to me was putting Yuri's disrespectful ass in her place.

"I'm really starting to get sick of you and ya bullshit! Since you got a mothafucking problem with me, how about we solve this shit right here right n—"

I barely finished my sentence before she ran up and punched me dead in the face. She hit me so hard that my bottom lip split wide open. I never even saw the shit coming even though I'd prompted her to do it.

Stumbling backwards, I grabbed my mouth in shock that she'd actually hit me. To keep it real, the only reason I'd started talking shit was because I didn't think she really would. Sadly, I was mistaken.

Yuri swung at me again, but I kicked the shit out of her big ass before her fist landed. She went hurdling backwards, crashing into two of her minions. The others quickly rushed in to join, and before I knew it, there was an all out war in the middle of the prison yard.

The fight barely lasted two minutes before the red alarm went off. Officers ran to back up their outnumbered colleagues, who were struggling to break up the altercation. Two of Yuri's girls were stomping the life out of me when the C.O.s pulled them off and forced them to the ground. Everyone else followed suit so that the officers didn't think they were involved too.

After the bitches were finally off me, I charged at Yuri full speed—but was quickly grabbed from behind by Mr. Asante. I felt like a ragdoll as he suspended me in mid-air with my arms and legs flailing wildly.

"I need you to calm down!" he yelled. "We have to get her to the infirmary! NOW!"

At first, I thought he was tripping over my busted lip until I noticed the shank hanging halfway out of my chest.

2

DIANA

Seven stitches and the possibility of being sent to the SHU were the consequences I faced all because I'd allowed a bitch to get under my skin. I still couldn't believe Yuri had actually stabbed me. A filed toothbrush with a razor blade melted in the end was what the nurse had pulled out of me. She told me that if it'd gone an inch deeper, it would have punctured my heart.

As I lay on the cold, stiff bed in the infirmary, I couldn't help but wish she'd killed me to save me from the thirty-year prison sentence I had to serve. Lost in thought, I didn't hear the door to my room open. Mr. Asante made his presence known by clearing his throat.

Quickly sitting up in bed, I tried my best to look as if I weren't in a considerable amount of pain. The last thing I wanted was someone seeing how weak and mentally exhausted I truly was—especially him.

"How you feelin'?" he asked with genuine concern. There was sadness in his eyes as he stared at me from across the room. Almost like he felt sorry for me.

Mr. Asante and I were all alone, save for the camera in the top right corner of the room and whoever was watching behind it.

"I've had better days...But hey, I'm alive so I can't complain..."

His frown darkened as he looked at me in a disapproving way. I could see it all in his eyes. He thought I was trouble. Because of the way he was staring at me, I shifted around nervously. Something about him caused me to feel intimidated. Perhaps it was the fact that he was fine as fuck.

Try as I might, I couldn't quite read his expression and that alone left me frustrated. "Why you looking at me like that?" I asked annoyed, not wanting to admit that he was making me uncomfortable.

There was no doubt in my mind that if he gazed at me for a second longer, I'd cream in my panties. The man was just that damn sexy, and it pained me to know that I hadn't had any dick in over a year.

Mr. Asante cocked his head a little and said, "I just don't understand what's so damn hard about doing ya time and going home? Why make your stay any more difficult than it has to be?"

"You think *I'm* making shit difficult?" I scoffed in amusement. "I'm not the one stabbing myself in the fucking chest."

"And why did she do that?" he asked casually, as if shanking me wasn't a big deal.

My mouth tightened. I almost was foolish

enough to answer but there was a strict no snitching policy when it came to the guards that us inmates took very seriously. "Doesn't matter..."

"I have to file an incident report...so actually it does—"

"I don't wanna talk about it, so just drop it already. Damn."

He remained calm despite my bad attitude. "Look, I can't help you if you don't help me."

The silence swelled ominously. I looked away to avoid eye contact with him and folded my arms. I didn't want his fucking help or sympathy. What I wanted was to get the fuck up out of prison...but I knew he couldn't help with that.

"I'm not the enemy, Diana," he said, staring meditatively at me.

I shook my head and chuckled a little. "Yeah...well you ain't my buddy and you sure as shit ain't my friend either," I reminded him, reiterating one of his earlier lines.

There was a brief moment of silence between us before he finally spoke again. "Just so you know, they wanted you in the SHU immediately after your release. But I fought for you to go back to gen because from what I saw it looked like you were the victim."

I scoffed in disgust. The *victim*? Ha! So in other words, I looked like I was getting my ass kicked. "I didn't ask you to do that," I said, cynically.

"And I didn't ask for your gratitude. But you're welcome." And with that, he turned and walked out of the room.

3

MAGYC

Thick, pillowy clouds of marijuana had the entire inside of my Wraith foggy as hell. Drake's *"4 PM in Calabasas"* poured through the custom speakers. The shit I was blowing on was so strong that it had the whole block lit. Parked directly across the street from me was the home of my ex-girlfriend Roxie.

She'd recently moved from her midtown condo into a small, bungalow out in Decatur. I figured she needed more room for her daughter Rain to grow. Relocating was something we were supposed to do together, and the fact that she'd moved on without me was still fucking me up.

Roxie had left me months ago and I still couldn't get over that shit—hence the reason I was sitting outside of her crib like I was a mothafucking stalker. After our split, I promised to give her space but I failed to fall through on my word because it was so hard for me to let her go.

Honestly, Roxie was the best thing that ever happened to a nigga. She and Rain came into my life a few years ago and transformed me into a better man—only I couldn't quite be the man she needed me to be.

You see a mothafucka like me had his vices.

Drugs, money, and bitches.

I had a serious addiction to all three, which only seemed to stifle the relationship I had with my girl. As my woman, she wanted to come first, and she deserved to...but for some reason I had trouble treating her like she was my main priority. I would stay out all night, come home whenever I felt like it, and fuck whomever I pleased.

For an entire year Roxie put up with my shit before finally throwing in the towel. Lack of loyalty and constant run-ins with my baby mama had created a permanent wedge between us. To make matters worse, she was now fucking with another dude...Some Korean Kung Fu mothafucka who'd violated me by playing house with a family I still claimed as my own. Roxie may've moved on but I damn sure hadn't. Once you fucked with me, you were stuck with me.

As if on cue, she walked out of the crib with a carrier and oversized Louis Vuitton bag in tow. I'd gotten it for her as a gift last Christmas and it was nice to see she still kept the shit I'd bought her. Maybe she was still holding on to certain memories of me as well.

As I watched her walk to her car, I noticed how care-free and happy she seemed. Suddenly, I doubted that she thought about me at all. I wouldn't have been surprised if she'd put me completely out of her mind. After the way I treated her, I couldn't say that I blamed her.

Roxie was just about to climb in her Benz when she noticed me parked across the street. She automatically knew that it was me because I was the only nigga in the 'hood pushing a matte black Wraith with peanut butter guts and 26" custom made rims. My cars always matched my personality; bold, black and extravagant.

Even though she recognized me, Roxie tried to front like I wasn't even there. Out of sight, out of mind.

Securing Rain in the backseat, she carried on about her business in a way that began to make me doubt my own existence. It was like I was invisible to her, and it fucked me up to know I'd taken her to that point.

Ashing my blunt, I opened the driver's door and climbed out. Luckily, I caught up with her just before she hopped in her whip. Roxie seemed annoyed by my mere presence as I approached her.

"Wassup, Rox?" She tried to pretend like she didn't hear me. "So you can't talk now? You antisocial?"

"I'm not anti-social. I'm just socially selective. There's a difference."

"Damn. When did it get so bad to where we can't even be cordial to one another?" I asked.

Roxie folded her arms and curved her lips in disgust. "When you started lying, cheating, and keeping shit from me."

She would never forgive me for keeping my son a secret. For her, it was a major deal breaker in addition to the baby mama drama she had to deal with on the regular. That, on top of the constant infidelities, was just too much for her to bear and she bounced on my ass.

Roxie tried to climb in the car but I quickly slammed the door shut. I could tell from her body language that she still wasn't fucking with me. "Why can't I ever get any of ya time?"

"Because you haven't earned it!" she snapped. "Last time we saw each other you was ready for a street brawl—"

"I was just acting out of emotions. I'm good now. I done got my shit together."

"Yeah...I bet you did now that it's convenient for you."

All of a sudden, Rain started crying in the backseat. Roxie tried to open the back door to get to her but I quickly trapped her in between my arms.

"Move, Magyc! Gotdamn, I have to get Rain." She tried to push me but I didn't budge an inch. "Watch out! Why you trying to smother me? You acting crazy."

"How the fuck you expect me to act seeing you with some other nigga?"

Roxie was so short that she barely came to my chest and she was at least fifty pounds lighter. She couldn't get pass me no matter how hard she tried and I definitely wasn't about to let her. I was determined for her to hear everything I had to say, because I couldn't go another month—another day—another minute without her. She and Rain were my life.

"I expect you to act like a damn adult. Not like some childish ass little bitch that can't control his feelings."

I decided to give Roxie a pass with that one, but on any other occasion I would've fucked her ass up. She knew how I felt about being disrespect and she still loved trying me.

Roxie was obviously still in her feelings about the night I caught up with her and Kwon in the parking lot of a diner they were leaving. I couldn't take seeing her with another man so I overreacted. She should've been thankful I didn't blow his mothafucking brains out on the spot.

To be honest, my problem wasn't the fact that he was Asian. He could've been any fucking ethnicity and I would've still acted the same way. My issue with him was that I felt like he was stepping on my toes.

Roxie still belonged to me. Regardless of her kicking me out her crib, turning down my marriage proposal, and blocking me on Instagram. None of that shit mattered. In my mind, I was still her nigga—and I wasn't going to let anybody get in the way of that. Letting another man ease into my old position was not happening. At least not while I was alive and breathing. I'd lose my mind before I lose my bitch.

"Stop running 'round with these lames and maybe I won't be so fucked up off my feelings."

"Who I choose to run around with ain't none of your business, Magyc."

"Every mothafucking thing that involves you is my business!"

"Who the fuck said we involved!" she yelled, causing Rain to cry even harder.

Roxie tried to get past me to console her, but I wouldn't let her by. Nothing was more important to me than making her see shit my way.

"Magyc, move! Damn!" Roxie whined in an unusually high-pitched voice that she normally used whenever she didn't feel like playing. "Get the fuck out of my way and let me get my baby!"

Roxie pushed me hard, and I grabbed her wrists and jerked her towards me. When she tried to put up a fight, I held her tighter in my embrace, reveling in the way her luscious body felt against mine.

Before she could say anything else, I crushed my lips against hers in hunger and desperation. For a split second, Roxie gave in...but in an instant it was over. Pushing me off her, she turned around and opened the back door to check on Rain. Her pacifier had fallen out her mouth and that was the only reason she was fussing. Rain was spoiled and to keep it real, it was partially my fault. When I was with Roxie I had treated her like she was my own...She still was.

"Can I at least see and spend some time with her every once in a while?" I asked Roxie after Rain finally settled down. I didn't give a fuck if she wasn't biologically mine. She was my daughter regardless.

"Why?" she asked with an attitude.

"Fuck you mean why? 'Cuz she's my kid—"

"She's not your kid, Magyc. You already have a kid, remember...with a bitch you couldn't stop fucking with while we were together."

Mentioning my baby mama, Tara was an all-time low blow. Roxie loved pushing my mothafucking buttons.

"Ya'll got ya'll own little thing going. We good over here," she said.

I chuckled in amusement. "Oh you good, huh?"

"Yeah...We're great."

Roxie tried to climb in the car but I stopped her again. I was just about to lay it on thick when I noticed a silver G wagon pull into her driveway.

Who the fuck is this?

My question was answered the moment I saw the slanted eyed mothafucka behind the steering wheel. He and two other people were inside the vehicle, and as soon as I recognized him jealousy manifested in the pit of my soul.

That mothafucka is gon' meet his maker fucking around...on that fuck shit.

"Why in the fuck is *he* here?" I questioned her.

Before Roxie could answer, Kwon hopped out with a confrontational look in his eyes. Dude wasn't feeling me at his girl's crib. That much was obvious. But if he wanted to get rid of me, he damn sure had to do something about it. Plain and simple.

"Is everything good?" Kwon asked Roxie.

Hearing him say that shit instantly set me off. *Why's he asking her if she's good. Ain't like I did shit to her.* "Why *wouldn't* she be good?" I answered for her.

Kwon took two bold steps towards me. "Because if it *was* a problem, I'm here to handle it."

Sensing that something was amidst, his friends climbed out of the truck as well. One was female and the other male. The guy was twice my size, but he could still catch this fade.

"Everything cool?" he asked Kwon.

Kwon looked from me to Roxie. "I don't know...Is it?"

"What'chu think, fuck nigga—"

My sentence was cut short when Kwon swiftly placed a razor sharp blade to my throat. He was so quick on the draw that I didn't even see him pull out the small machete. The fifteen-inch knife was so close that I could feel the stainless steel pressing into my Adam's apple. A tiny sliver of blood ran down my neck and onto my Armani t-shirt.

"Kwon! Oh my God—WHAT THE FUCK?!" Roxie screamed, causing Rain to cry again.

Neither one of us saw that shit coming.

"Have you lost your mind?!" Roxie quickly stepped up in my defense and Kwon looked over at her like he didn't understand why she was tripping.

The minute he took his eyes off me, I pulled out my glock and pressed the barrel to his temple.

"Ya'll gon' do this shit right here? Right now?!" she asked in disbelief.

Kwon and I held our weapons stagnant despite her pleas. I wanted to blow his head off as bad as he wanted to slit my throat. Jealousy and resentment had somehow led us here.

"Magyc!" Roxie yelled...but when I didn't budge, she turned to Kwon and called his name. "So ya'll really gon' do this shit in front of my baby?!" she cried.

Hearing her mention Rain quickly snapped me back to reality. Against my better judgment, I slowly lowered my gun first out of respect for Roxie and her daughter. But if they weren't present, there was nothing on earth that would've stopped me from killing his bitch ass.

Kwon hesitantly followed suit even though I was sure he wanted to end me where I stood. Two hot headed niggas fighting over the same bitch was a bad combination.

"This shit ain't over," I told him, letting him know just how serious I was about mine. "You can believe that. We gon' see each other again..."

"I'll be waiting," Kwon said, watching me leave.

In misery, I climbed in my car and peeled off with my heart still in her possession. The wall Roxie had built up between us was impenetrable, and I had to do something major—and fast if I planned on winning her back.

4
ROXIE

"Where the fuck did that come from?! I never seen you act like that! Just when I felt like I was getting to know you, you show me a side of you that I never knew existed!" I went off on Kwon the second Magyc pulled off. This was a part of him that I'd never seen before. I felt like I was looking at a stranger. And it was a shame too, because when Kwon and I first met, I really thought that he was the one for me.

Kind, caring, funny, cute, and down-to-earth, he was everything I wanted in a partner and more. He was damn near perfection...until today. Until today, I had no idea that he had a dark side to him as well. Hell, I'd never even noticed that he carried a small machete around.

"And you're wielding a mothafucking knife too? Like really—what the fuck are you thinking? I feel like I don't even know you!"

Kwon tucked his knife back into its holster before casually pulling his shirt over it. "Everyone has their means of protecting themselves," he said. "Mine are just a little unconventional."

"*Unconventional?*" I repeated. "You call putting a blade to my ex's throat in broad daylight unconventional?"

"He put a gun to my head."

"Yeah...After you put a knife to his," I reminded him. "I mean, what were you thinking—"

"I was thinking that I had enough of him disrespecting us," he said. "Do you not remember what happened in the parking lot a few months back? I've had it up to here with his shit. You two have been over for a while now, and he still keeps sniffing around. What the hell was he doing here anyway?" There was a slight edge to his tone that I wasn't at all used to hearing.

"I could ask you the same thing. I thought we were supposed to meet at the movie theater." I felt no inclination to give him an explanation right then.

I'd agreed to a double date, and was on my way to the theater when Magyc popped up unexpectedly. How was I supposed to know that Kwon would show up on the scene as well?

"I changed my mind. Plus, I needed to see you sooner," he said, pulling me towards him.

As angry as I was with him, a smile still formed on my lips. He was sexy enough to suck me right into his game. Kwon had smooth ivory skin, a square jaw, small kissable lips, a cut in his left brow, and dark hooded eyes that were seductive by default. He was an uncommonly handsome man.

Kwon was fresh to death that day in a pair

of fitted jeans, black V-neck, and matching Louis Vuitton belt and scarf. On his feet were $1200 Damier-patterned sneaker boots, and accentuating the entire fit was a white faced Rolex valued at more than $38,000. His clothes and swag echoed his general demeanor.

Damn. I still can't believe I don't know what this dude does for a living.

Biting my bottom lip, I forced my mouth into a smile "Oh, you need me now, huh?" I asked with a sly grin.

Kwon slid his hands into the back pocket of my jeans and kissed my forehead as I hummed a terrible rendition of Rihanna's *"Needed Me"*.

He gave me a charming smile and said, "You know I do...Or else I wouldn't be ready to cut a motherfucker's throat open." Kwon laughed a little, making his threat sound a bit less heinous. "I know you said it's over between you two... But I feel like it's hard for us to move forward when *he* hasn't even moved on."

In an effort to take his mind off my ex, I cupped Kwon's face and stared deep into his brown eyes. "Let's not dwell on the past," I told him. "Because that's all it is."

Kwon lifted a brow in skepticism. "*Is* that all it is?" he asked doubtfully.

I gave him a kiss for reassurance. "That's *all* it is."

"I don't believe you," he said.

"I don't believe you're really acting like you're threatened by another man. An ex at that," I told him. "Lack of confidence doesn't suit you."

Kwon's cheeks turned bright red, and his left eye twitched a little.

"Like I said, the past is the past."

And I meant every word of that. Even though I loved Magyc and the way he treated my daughter, I couldn't go backwards. I'd done everything to get that nigga out of my system, including deleting all things related to him. I didn't want to open that door again

I was still disgusted by him and his deceiving, manipulative ways. He was sloppy as fuck and too much drama. I wasn't ready to go through that shit again. Magyc and I were over, and there was no going back.

My mother always told me *'those without a vision for their future return to the past'*. And right now, Kwon was my present and my future.

***

Me, Kwon, and his friends made it to the Regal Cinema in record time for the previews. After piling up on junk food, we all entered the crowded screening room to watch the new *Captain America* movie.

As we took our seats, Kwon handed me a pair of 3D glasses and a pack of fruit snacks. I had just gotten comfortable when the entire room went totally black. Reclining my seat just a little, I prepared to enjoy a flick that I'd heard wonderful things about.

"Thanks for making time for me today," he whispered. "I know in between working and being a mom, spare time comes far and few. I appreciate you spending some of it with me. Means a lot."

"Oh, Kwon. You know it's never an inconvenience. I love spending time with you."

Kwon smiled and kissed the back of my hand. I blushed a little, surprised that he still had that effect on me even though we'd been seeing each other a while now.

"I love spending time with you too," he said. "Matter of fact, I wouldn't mind spending every day with you...for the rest of my life."

All of a sudden, a series of words appeared on the screen that were completely unrelated to film in general. Written in bold lettering on the projection screen were the words:

ROXIE...I know by agreeing to this, you'd be taking a huge risk...but I guarantee it'll be one you won't regret. Meeting you has changed my whole world and the way that I view it. You complete me. And it would make me the happiest man in the world if you were my wife...Please accept my hand in marriage.

The entire room erupted in cheers and applause as my stomach clenched into a little knot. When I looked to my left, Kwon had a small black velvet box in his hand with the lid lifted. Resting inside the satin slit was a sparkling 24-carat diamond princess cut engagement ring.

My mouth fell open in shock. I was at a complete loss for words. Tears slowly filled my eyes as a flurry of emotions washed over me. In that moment, I was too emotional to even speak, and the only thing I could do was cry.

5
ROXIE

The ride back home was silent and filled with tension following the proposal at the movie theater. I'd crushed Kwon's spirit after turning down his offer for marriage, and though it pained me to do so, I knew that I'd made the right decision.

Even though I did see potential for a future with Kwon, I wasn't quite sure that I was ready to spend the rest of my life with him. We were still getting to know one another...And after his little display with Magyc earlier, I wasn't really sure that I knew him at all.

"I think you should reconsider..." Kwon's rigid tone was laced with bitterness and disappointment. Steering the G wagon, he shook his head in despair.

I could tell that he wasn't expecting me to say no. No one wanted to be turned down, especially after such a carefully thought out proposal. He'd put so much effort into making me feel as if he wanted me to become his wife, and for a second, I did. But then I thought about it...and realized that if I agreed, I'd probably be making one of the biggest mistakes of my life.

Kwon and I had only been dating for a few months. Hell, we'd never even met each other's parents before. In my opinion, we didn't know enough about one another to take such a huge step.

"How do you know I haven't?"

Kwon took his eyes off the road for a second to look at me. "*Today*? How could you have reconsidered when I just proposed today? Now you're just talking crazy."

"I'm not talking crazy, you acting crazy. Pulling knives and shit—I didn't even know you were capable of something like that before today. I just started bringing you around my daughter. Not to mention, I still don't even know what you do for a living! It's so many things you're revealing to me day by day. I know this is not what you wanna hear, but we're just not ready."

6

KWON

I was surprisingly able to hold my composure during the short drive back to Roxie's place despite the fact that I was fuming mad inside. Fate had just dealt a terrible blow. I couldn't believe that she'd actually turned down my marriage proposal. Her answer wasn't a sufficient explanation, and I couldn't accept it coming from her. Not after everything we'd been through.

I loved Roxie. Her dark skin, sparkling eyes, and luminous smile made my heart beat faster every time she was near. I accepted everything about her that made her who she was—including her flaws. And I loved that she accepted me. We were perfect for each other. There wasn't another woman on the face of this planet I wanted more than her. Roxie was made for me.

I'd thought she felt the same way but apparently that wasn't the case. I had so much faith in her agreeing to marry me that I even planned an after party to celebrate the news. Sadly, the celebration would have to be canceled.

This was one of the worst days of my life.

Honestly, after the run-in with her ex, I was a little skeptical about going through with it...but I was confident that she'd say yes regardless. Now I felt like a total ass for going out on a limb.

How the fuck could she turn me down like that? And in front of all those people? In front of my friends?

I silently cursed myself. I would never forget the sheer embarrassment I felt or the sympathetic look in everyone's eyes as they stared at me. As a man, Roxie wouldn't understand what that did to my pride. My dignity was offended.

It was the unfortunate consequence of assuming. Assuming that Roxie loved me as much as I loved her. Assuming she cared about me like I cared about her. Assuming she was ready to take my last name and start a new life with me.

Boy, was I fucking wrong.

When I finally pulled into the driveway of Roxie's crib, I couldn't even make eye contact with her to say goodnight. I was just that hurt and humiliated. A man of my status didn't handle rejection well.

In my world, the word 'no' was not something I heard often, and being turned down was not something that I was used to. In my world, I got whatever I wanted with no objections. And right now, I wanted Roxie— more than anything I'd ever wanted in life. Knowing she didn't want me in the same way fucked my shit all the way up.

After dropping Roxie off, I headed straight to the hotel I'd been living out of during my stay in Atlanta. I was in my feelings so much that I didn't even bother kissing her and Rain goodbye like I normally did. I simply wanted to put some distance between us so that she didn't see how bad she'd really hurt me.

Valet quickly came to collect my truck when I reached the hotel. My mind was heavy as I made my way up to my penthouse suite on the 30th floor. My business phone vibrated in my pocket but answering it wasn't a priority.

Once I reached my room, I saw two suited men standing on either side of my door— each one on my payroll. I always kept a pair of killers wherever I laid my head. And when I was out and about, I had Sara and Kim with me, who were the couple that had accompanied us to the movies.

For months, Roxie was under the impression that they were just my friends but really they were trained assassins hired to protect me. And I never left home without protection. My killers might not have always been in plain view, but they were always with me...like guardian angels.

"Evening sir. May I have a word with you," the tallest of the duo asked.

"Not now," I replied through my teeth.

"But sir, I have unfortunate news—"

I quickly raised my hand dismissively. "I said not now."

He graciously apologized just as I Inserted the keycard into my door. Stepping inside, I slammed it shut behind me, causing the picture frames on the wall to rattle. I didn't have time for any more bad news. I was still mad as fuck about Roxie turning me down in front of everyone. I was appallingly embarrassed.

In a sudden fit of rage, I kicked the nearby chair halfway across the room, leaving a dent behind in the nearby wall. I wasn't worried about the damages or cost of repairs. If I wanted to, I could've easily bought the whole mothafucking Ritz.

Seething with fury, I went on a complete tirade, trashing my entire hotel room and breaking anything in sight. I kicked over tables, tossed trashcans at the wall, and even destroyed the television. When my pocket continued to vibrate, I snatched out the 24-carat gold iPhone and launched it at the window where it cracked upon impact.

Once I realized that trashing my room wasn't enough, I resorted to banging my head against the wall. Over the years, my violent outbursts had become increasingly uncontrollable.

I'd stopped taking meds to control my

temper a long time ago.

WHAM!

WHAM!

WHAM!

I continued bashing my skull against the surface of the wall until it split open and leaked blood.

BOOM!

BOOM!

BOOM!

"Sir, is everything okay?" the same security guard called out. He sounded concerned because of all the noise. "Sir, I really need to speak with you—"

"Just leave me the fuck alone!"

"Sir...you really need to hear this."

Angered by his persistence and inability to follow directions, I ran towards the door, snatched it open and grabbed my machete. Before he could say another word, I sliced his throat wide open and watched as blood sprayed onto my designer t-shirt.

Grabbing his neck, he backed up in terror while trying his best to stop the bleeding but it was a pointless effort. Within seconds, he was on the ground, choking and taking his final ragged breaths. He should've listened when I told him to leave me be. Failing to comply had cost him his life.

The second guard made no effort whatsoever to help his fallen comrade. He knew that if he did I would kill him too.

I watched as my victim's body went limp. His fingers twitched involuntarily.

"Take care of this mess and call the cleaners," I told the second guard.

"Yes sir," he obediently replied.

Wiping the blood out of my eye from the gaping wound on my head, I prepared to go back into my room—but stopped suddenly. "Oh...and one more thing."

"Yes sir?"

"Do not disturb me. I need this moment of solitude."

"Yes sir. Of course," he said in Korean.

Pleased with his compliance, I walked back into my room and closed the door behind me. Much to my surprise, the cellphone on the floor was still ringing regardless of its screen being cracked.

Despite what I'd just told my security guard, I knelt down and grabbed the phone anyway. Sinking into a nearby chair, I looked at the caller ID. It was my sister, Hae-Won. She was two years younger than me and served as second-in-command for our family business. She only called this line for emergencies so I knew that something had to be wrong.

Pressing the lime button, I placed the phone to my ear. Hae-Won quickly spoke before I had the chance to.

"We have a huge problem," she said in Korean. "I just got word that the police have infiltrated us."

7
DIANA

Mission one…

I'ma put this on…

When he see me in the dress I'ma get me some…

Mission two…

Gotta make that call…

Tell him get the bottles poppin' when they play my song…

Mission three…

Got my three best friends…

Like we do it all the time, we gon' do it again…

Mission four…

Got the vintage Rolls…

Drop a couple hundreds tell him leave it at the door…

I ain't worried doing me tonight…

A little sweat ain't never hurt nobody…

While ya'll standin' on the wall…

I'm the one tonight…

Getting bodied. Getting bodied. Getting bodied. Getting bodied…

Beyoncé's *"Get Me Bodied"* played on Nyri's tiny radio as I showed a group of girls in my pod how to twerk. Since I was the only former stripper among them, they all looked to me to teach them dance moves they would one day show their men upon release. Even though I wasn't getting out any time soon, I didn't mind because it was fun and a good way to stay active.

"How the fuck you make your ass move like that though? I feel so stiff when I do it," Bianca said, amateurishly shaking her butt.

"Bitch, you *look* stiff too," I laughed. "Here, bend your knees a little lower. Arch your back more. And just pop that shit."

Mission five…

Skip to the front of the line…

Let me fix my hair up 'fore I go inside…

Mission six…

Gotta check these chicks…

'Cause you know they gone block when I take these flicks…

Mission seven…

Gotta make my rounds…

Givin' eyes to the guys now I think I found him…

Mission eight…

Now we conversate…

And we can skip small talk let's get right to the chase...

Beyoncé crooned through the speakers as I continued twerking and shaking my ass like I was being paid to. All of this dancing actually made me miss the strip club. Now that I was locked up, I would've given anything to be back up on that stage, twirling around a tall metal pole. Truthfully, anywhere was better than being behind bars. But somehow I was able to make the best out of a bad situation thanks to my girls.

Speaking of friends, Nyri was twerking her ass off like a pro but only because I'd shown her how to months earlier. When the chorus to the song dropped again so did I. With no hands, I popped and danced like a flurry of bills where raining down on us.

From my peripheral, I caught Mr. Asante watching...but when we made eye contact, he quickly looked away. A smile tugged at my lips because I knew that he liked what he saw.

That nigga be giving me a hard time, but if the circumstances were different, I bet he'd be all over a bitch.

Little did I know, that statement would soon be put to the ultimate test.

***

The following afternoon was visitation and as usual, no guards came to get me or my roommate. Luckily, we had each other to keep company since it wasn't like anyone ever came to see us. We'd gotten so used to not having any visitors that we didn't even talk or entertain the thought. We were both in the same boat, having no friends or family to support us during our stay. But thankfully, we had one another as a support system. Without Nyri, I would've gone crazy a long time ago.

"Diana?" she called out from the bottom bunk. She was so quiet that for a second I thought she was sleeping.

Closing my book, I rolled over in bed. "Wassup, boo?"

"...Can I ask you a question?"

I laughed. "You just did."

That got a laugh out of her as well. "I'm serious."

"I'm just playing. Go right ahead."

Nyri paused before she continued. "If you could get revenge on the nigga and them bitches that set you up...would you?"

Nyri's question caught me off guard. I wasn't expecting to hear anything about those traitors, because honestly I tried my best to keep my mind off of them. If I spent every day harping on the reason why I was here, then surely I'd drive myself insane. Besides, there was no undoing what was already done.

"To be real...I don't even know..." I told

her.

"You don't know? What do you mean you don't know? After all the foul shit this mothafucka did to you? I would blow that mothafucka's head off."

Before I could respond, the door to our room opened and Mr. Asante poked his head inside. "Let's go Prince. You've got a visitor."

For a hot minute, I thought he'd mistaken me for someone else. "What? *Me*?" I asked in disbelief. No one ever came to see me.

"*Heyyy*, Mr. Asante," Nyri sang with a huge, flirty grin.

He ignored her, totally unfazed by the many flirtatious gestures he received on a daily basis. Giving me a look of pure irritation, he said, "Yes, you."

I still didn't budge. "Are you *sure* you have the right inmate?"

Finally fed up with me stalling, he prepared to leave. "You know what, come or stay. It doesn't really make a difference to me."

Because I was curious to see who my visitor was, I quickly hopped out the bunk. "Hold on! Wait up!" Mr. Asante stopped just before closing our door. The man had absolutely no patience. "I think I'll come."

Mr. Asante led me and a few other women to the prison visitation room where friends and relatives awaited our arrival. Once we reached the door and were permitted access, he left us to the armed guards who were stationed in each corner of the room.

My heart pounded with excitement as I scanned the many faces seated in hopes that one of them would either be Cameron or Roxie. Neither one of those bitches had came to see me or wrote me, and a visit from them was long overdue.

When I finally saw the person waiting for me at an empty table, I literally wanted to faint. My stomach clenched into a tiny knot and my cheeks flushed in anger. I felt like I was trapped in a nightmare. Was I really seeing this mothafucka right now or was I dreaming?

Rico cracked a grin that I desperately wanted to slap off of his face. The nerve of this bitch to show up a whole year after I'd gotten locked up. He was like a Herpes outbreak, popping up unexpectedly.

My feet somehow managed to move forward on their own, in spite of me being tempted to go back to my cell. It was as if my body had a mind of its own. Like obligation was the driving force behind my movement.

I wanted—no I needed to know why Rico let me take the fall. Hell, an explanation was the very least that I deserved, considering all the shit that he put me through.

There were no signs of happiness present as I slowly took a seat across from him. The intoxicating scent of his Creed cologne greeted me before he did. Rico looked even better than he smelled.

He sported a black tee, black fitted Balenciaga jeans, a Versace scarf, and gold Maison Margiela sneakers. Rico was finer than a mothafucka...but he was still a damn snake in disguise.

Rico had a complex occupation that involved dealing with dozens of girls. His hustle was on some next level shit. He only dealt with exotic women who were in the US temporarily for work purposes. His roster of girls consisted of the baddest broads from Brazil, the Philippines, Costa Rica, Thailand, Puerto Rico, Columbia, Africa, Barbados, and the Dominic Republic. After helping them obtain their work visas—which only lasted for a total of 90 days— he flew them out and showed them how to prosper.

"Why are you here?" I asked with obvious attitude.

"Can we talk?"

"Depends on if you have anything good to talk about."

"Take a seat, Diana," he said, gesturing towards the empty chair.

I complied—even though there was a

myriad of other things I wanted to do instead. Like beating his ass with a steel baseball bat or throwing sulfuric acid in his face. That was just how much I hated this nigga.

I couldn't believe there was once a time when I loved his dirty drawers. I used to be so intrigued by everything about him; from his looks, to his authoritative swag, to his dexterity. I used to hang onto every word he said. There was a wisdom about him that came from hanging around older niggas all of his life. His conversations had substance and aggression, and his demeanor shook the tallest of buildings.

I used to be crazy about him.

Now...I couldn't even stand the sight of his ass.

"Hey, baby," he smiled, reaching across the table. He wanted me to take his hands but all I did was stare at them. Tattooed on the back of his left one was the star and crescent and on his right was the Eye of Horus—an Egyptian symbol of protection and good health. "You looking good," he noted.

"And you're looking like you put on a couple pounds," I shot back.

Rico had always been chubby but he was a fat nigga with swag and even fatter pockets. Bitches loved him regardless of him being overweight. He was Moroccan with a dash of Seminole Indian so he had a good, wavy texture of hair and soft French vanilla skin. He had a full, thick beard and a natural boss-like presence about him.

Rico licked his lips. "I thought you was a woman who liked everything big."

Leaning back in my chair, I folded my arms and snorted in disgust. "Why the fuck are you here, Rico? What makes you think I wanna see your fucking mug after everything you did to me?"

"Alright, baby. I'll take the blame."

"You damn sure right you will! YOU THE ONE WHO PUT ME IN THIS BITCH!"

"Inmate! Keep it down or I'll have you escorted back to the unit! This is your first and final warning," a nearby C.O. threatened.

"You let me take the fall for ya'll asses!" I hissed, in a much quieter tone. "Then you had your bitches get up on the stand and testify against me. I lost my freedom, my baby— *everything*, because of you! And you got the nerve to say you'll take the mothafucking blame? You got me fucked up on so many levels! Who the fuck else would I blame?"

Rico kept his composure despite my harsh words and blatant disrespect. "Are you done?" he asked calmly.

"What the fuck do you mean am I done—"

"I've heard you out. Now it's your turn to

listen to me."

"Yeah well, I hope and pray you have something good to say. Because I'm literally two seconds from getting the fuck up and walking out." I then gave him a chance to explain but as soon as he opened his mouth I cut him off. "How could you do this to me?" I cried. "I loved you!" I could no longer hold it in and all of my emotions came pouring out.

"I loved you too, Diana—I still do. But we gotta code we live by. And it's a code that should never be violated."

"Well, I'm violating the fuck outta your code right now, 'cuz I don't give a fuck! What about my freedom? What about the thirty years I'll never get back? What about the child I lost?" Tears ran down my cheeks. I was an emotional wreck. "How could you do this shit to me, Rico? *To me!*" I patted my chest. "Of all people? Somebody you claim to love? Somebody who trusted you! I trusted you!" I said, pointing a finger in his face. "Somebody that had your mothafucking back. Everything you ever told me was bullshit! You never gave two shits about me—"

"You know that's a lie—"

"Bullshit!"

"You mean everything to me. Shit, just me being here shows you how much I care. And if I care about you, you have power over me. And trust me, that ain't something easily obtained."

"Yeah, whatever. That shit sounds real convincing coming from a nigga who ain't came to see me in over a year." My tone was dripping with sarcasm. "You obviously don't care that gotdamn bad."

Rico shrugged his shoulders. "I had to let shit die down. You know how it is."

His answer wasn't good enough for me, and all it did was make me want to slap the shit out of him. I didn't know anyone who was more heartless and selfish than him. Rico was Satan reincarnated. I'd fucked around and gotten a taste of hell, and now I was paying dearly for it.

"I *thought* I knew how it was. Hell, I thought I knew a lot of shit." The fact that Rico had abandoned me showed me just how little I knew about him.

I'd foolishly believed that I could trust him when in reality he was only using me. Scheming behind my back and prematurely plotting on my downfall. I was so wrong about him and truthfully, I deserved everything that came with my poor decision making.

Why are you even here?" I asked for the third time.

Rico clasped his hands together and smiled. "I'm here because I have good news. And I wanted to be the first one to share it."

"*Good news*? Are you serious?" I laughed only because he sounded ridiculous. "What good could *possibly* come out your fucking mouth?"

"Well...for starters, me and my legal team have been working on getting your charges exonerated. If we succeed, you could be looking at an automatic prison release," he explained. "How's that for good news?"

8
DIANA

When I made it back to my cell, I felt a multitude of emotions. Apart of me was happy about the news that Rico had given me, but on the other hand, I was still pissed about him putting me in this fucked up predicament. If I'd never gotten involved with his sheisty ass, I wouldn't even be here in the first place.

Just him coming here was like a slap in my face. And now he was telling me that *he* was the key to my freedom. Truthfully, I didn't want to deal with his ass—but if he was telling the truth then I had no other choice but to.

I felt like I was trapped in between a rock and a hard place. *How could this nigga put me in this place and then tell me he's the only one who can get me out?* Was this his clever way of saving me so that I could forever be indebted to him?

I wasn't sure.

But one thing I was certain of was that I couldn't trust Rico. Not now. Not ever.

"Wassup, D? Is everything cool?" Nyri asked, sitting up in bed. She sensed that something was wrong the minute I entered our cell. "I take it the visit didn't go so well."

Tears filled my eyes as I shook my head. "I'm okay," I lied—even though inside, I was falling apart. My mind was everywhere. I couldn't even think straight.

"You're not okay. Talk to me."

Suddenly, I broke down crying. I could no longer suppress my heartache and sadness. Nyri quickly climbed out of her bed to console me but changed her mind after I kicked our toilet. I was so angry, bitter, and emotional, and I needed to exude that pent up frustration someway somehow.

"WHO THE FUCK DOES HE THINK HE IS?!" I hollered at no one in particular. Rico had some nerve even showing his fucking face. Just seeing him stirred up a mixture of feelings that I had struggled to bury long ago.

"Calm down, D. What's wrong? What happened?" Nyri questioned.

Before I could answer, a female officer opened our door and poked her head in. She must've heard the loud bang. "What seems to be the problem in here?"

The fact that she was intruding pissed me off and I just snapped. "YOU'RE MY MOTHAFUCKING PROBLEM!" I screamed. "Why the fuck is you even here?! I mean shit! Am I not allowed to get angry? Am I not allowed to vent?! Am I not allowed to act human? GOTDAMN! For fuck's sake, just leave me the fuck alone!" She felt all of my anguish as I took my frustrations out on her.

"That's it! You're coming with me!" she said, grabbing me roughly. The callow officer had no other solution than to throw me in the SHU. "You can vent all you want in the security housing unit. How does that sound?"

Upon hearing all the chaos, Mr. Asante stepped inside. "What's going on in here?" he asked.

"Inmate Prince here needs time to cool off in solitary."

"Don't worry. I got it from here," he said, reaching for me. Because he was chief officer, she agreed to handing me over, although I could tell she wasn't happy about it.

Mr. Asante led me out of the room by my arm like a parent would his child. As we left the pod, I mentally prepared myself for a lengthy stay in the SHU. But halfway there, he took a detour to the prison yard instead.

"Why am I here?" I asked him.

Mr. Asante finally released me. "You tell me," he said. "What was all that shit back there?"

"Look, I had a moment, aight. I got upset and flipped out. It wasn't like I was hurting anybody. She was just being a bitch—"

"No, she was just doing her job," he corrected me.

Folding my arms, I sighed and shook my head in misery.

Mr. Asante must've saw the stress in my eyes because he offered me a Newport. Normally, I didn't smoke cigarettes but considering my current state of affairs, I graciously accepted. Because only God knew the next time I would get another opportunity.

Mr. Asante was kind enough to light the end for me, and for the first time, I realized that he wasn't all that bad.

"Thanks..." I muttered before taking a long pull.

He fired up one as well and for several seconds we simply smoked in silence.

The fresh air was just what I needed to calm down because the visit with Rico had me feeling some type of way.

"I never took you for a smoker," I said, breaking the silence.

"To be real, I only do it when I'm at work."

"Why's that?" I asked. "Wifey don't want you smoking the house out?" It was my slick way of trying to see if he had a significant other.

Mr. Asante gave me a discerning look. He knew exactly what I was trying to do and he wasn't falling for my trap. "How 'bout we talk about you," he said.

"What about me do you wanna talk about?" There was a hint of flirtation in my tone. I couldn't help myself with a man this fine.

"Well...for starters...why's it so hard to stay out of trouble?" he asked.

"I don't go looking for trouble. Trouble usually finds me."

"And why's that?"

I tore my gaze away from the barbed wire fence to look at him. "I don't know... Maybe 'cuz of things I've done in my past."

"Is that what got'chu actin' out of character today? Your *past*?"

I knew that he was referring to my visit with Rico. "Something like that," I answered smugly.

"Well, my father always told me 'only a fool trips on what's behind him'."

9
ROXIE

Later on that night, Kwon surprised me with an unexpected visit. I had just laid Rain down for the night when I heard "*Father Stretch My Hands*" blasting in the driveway. The only reason I knew that it was him was because Yeezy was his favorite rapper.

"This nigga gon' wake my baby up if he don't turn that bullshit down."

After quietly closing the door to Rain's room, I switched to the front of the house with irritation emanating from me. Lately, he'd made a habit out of popping up uninvited and truthfully, I couldn't quite say that I was fond of it. Kwon and I were still in the beginning stages of our relationship, and there were some barriers that shouldn't have been crossed. Like visiting without calling first.

As soon as I swung the front door open, Kwon turned off the engine and climbed out of his gold Porsche GT3. It seemed like every other day he was pushing a new luxury rental, which only increased my curiosity about his means of income.

When Kwon looked up at me and smiled, all of my irritation quickly dissipated. He was so damn handsome that I forgot why I was mad. Kwon was dressed in a white Comme Des

Garçons tee, black fitted jeans that were torn at the knees, and red Versace sneakers. He screamed perfection, even with the small band-aid on his forehead.

Damn. Why the fuck he gotta be so mothafucking fine?

Kwon casually made his way towards me, bringing with him a sweet scent of Italian deodorant and Hermés cologne. "To what do I owe the pleasure of this unexpected visit?" I asked. "And what happened to your head?"

Kwon brusquely walked past me inside the house. "Where's Rain? We need to start packing. We don't have much time."

"Wait. What are you talking about?" I asked, running after him.

Kwon ignored me as he barged inside my bedroom and snatched my suitcase out of the closet. I figured he'd gotten into some trouble as I watched him carelessly toss clothes inside. He made me feel like we were on the run.

"What is going on, Kwon? You're low-key scaring me!"

"I don't have time to explain. Just get Rain. I already have a private aircraft on its way. We have to go...now!"

"Go where?! And why?"

"Back to Korea. I have important business matters that I need to tend to."

"And what does that have to do with me and my daughter?"

"I don't know how long I'll be there. This matter could require a lot of time to handle and I don't want us thousands of miles away from each other."

After tossing a heaping of clothes inside my suitcase, he slammed it shut and walked past me towards Rain's room. He was just about to go inside when I stopped him.

"And how do you know I wanna be thousands of miles away from home?" I asked. "You're talking about this business you gotta handle but I still don't even know what the fuck you do. You can't expect me to just uproot myself and my daughter when you can't even be honest with me."

Kwon sighed in frustration. "Roxie, I don't have time for this right now—"

"And I don't have time to leave town. How 'bout that?"

"In time, you'll know just what's going on...but right now we gotta get out of here—"

"Tell me why!" I demanded. Warm tears ran down my cheeks as I begged for the truth. I needed it more than anything.

"I can't do that..." he said.

"Then neither can I."

Kwon looked defeated as he stood there

in utter silence. I was giving him an ultimatum; a decision—the truth for my trust.

In the end, he decided that keeping secrets was far more important than being real. With nothing left to say, he walked right past me and left out of the house, slamming the door behind him. In that moment, it had never been more clear to me that Kwon was not the one for me.

10
DIANA

Nyri and I were forking through the slop they served for lunch when Bianca joined us at our table. "Heads up, D...word in the streets is that your girl's getting out today. And you know that clitty-licker gon' be looking to get even too, so you better watch ya back."

Bianca couldn't have delivered worse news....

"Are you kidding me? She's barely been in the SHU for two whole weeks!" Nyri said. "I can't believe they really letting that crazy bitch out! She tried to kill you! How the fuck could they take that shit lightly?"

"You know how," Bianca said. "These mothafuckas don't care about us! When you gon' wake up and realize that shit?"

Nyri cast a nervous glance my way. I could tell that she wasn't looking forward to the drama that was sure to come. Neither was I.

Glancing around the congested cafeteria, I noticed a few of Yuri's girls mean-mugging me. The war was already underway.

"Shit," I muttered.

I wasn't even fully healed yet and they were already releasing this bitch back into general population. If I didn't know any better, I'd think they were trying to get me murdered.

"*Psst*," Bianca whispered.

I looked down to see what she was passing me underneath the table and saw that it was a shank. "Bianca, I can't—"

"Just take it!" she instructed. "Shit, you never know. You just might need it..."

***

A few hours after lunch, Mr. Asante came to collect me from my cell for a check-in with the nurse since I was due to have my sutures removed. Yuri had yet to return to gen but I still kept my guards up as I anxiously awaited her arrival. In the meantime, I would enjoy the peace that her absence brought. Besides, I knew that it wouldn't last very long.

Mr. Asante and I were walking through the hallway alone when I decided to state the obvious. "The scars on your face. How did you get them?"

Mr. Asante didn't respond until we finally reached the nurse's office. "Doesn't matter. What'chu oughta be focused on is how you gon' stay outta trouble," he said before opening the door for me.

I gave him a sly grin before murmuring, "If you have any trouble, it won't be outta me."

After my wound was dressed and my stitches were removed, a different C.O. came to get me since Mr. Asante was on lunch break. When I entered the pod, everyone was out of their cells for rec.

It didn't take long for me to notice that something was different in the atmosphere. All of the women were either staring at me strangely or avoiding me altogether. It was like I had leprosy or some shit.

A few seconds later, I realized why everyone was acting so weird. My least favorite person had finally returned to the unit. Leaning against the wall, Yuri and her girls watched my every move. They were ready to get it popping.

Luckily, so was I.

Reaching behind my back, I made sure that the shank Bianca had given me was still there.

It was.

Speaking of Bianca, she and Nyri were watching me from across the pod as I walked cautiously to my cell. The nervous looks on their faces made me feel even more uneasy. There was so much tension in the air, that everyone in the unit sensed it.

After disappearing inside my cell for several minutes, I emerged with a hardcover copy of *"A Game of Thrones."*

As soon as I entered the rec room to read, I noticed that all of the cameras had been turned out of view, and all of the C.O.s that were once present was now gone. It didn't take a genius to figure out that they'd been paid to disappear.

All of a sudden, a woman jumped up in anger, causing the chair she was seated in to fall over. "BITCH, WHO THE FUCK YOU THINK YOU TALKING TO?!" she screamed.

I was so caught off guard by the confrontation that I didn't notice Yuri running straight at me with a shank in her hand. Before I could realize that it was all just a distraction, she jammed her blade deep inside me.

"AHHH!"

Surprised by the attack, I fell to the floor with a hard thud. Yuri quickly climbed on top on me and stabbed me repeatedly in the chest.

11

DIANA

Everyone in the pod looked on in horror as Yuri viciously stabbed me over and over again. In my peripheral, I noticed Nyri running over to help—but was quickly thwarted by a group of bull daggers. Suddenly, my life flashed before my very eyes. This big ass bitch was really about to kill me!

When I raised my hand to push her off, she sliced the shit out of all five fingers. Remembering that I had Bianca's shank, I went to grab it—but realized that it'd been knocked off of me.

"Bitch, where the fuck you think you going? You ain't going nowhere! You gon' die right here on this floor!" Yuri yelled.

From the corner of my eye, I noticed my book laying several feet away. Desperately reaching for it, I grabbed the hardcover and smashed it against her temple.

Caught off guard by the assault, Yuri fell over and grabbed her head. I gave her no time to recuperate as I hopped on top of her and started raining blow after devastating blow. I was savage in my attack, connecting with every part of her body that I could reach. This bitch just wouldn't stop coming for me. Now I had to take matters into my own hands to ensure that she never tried this shit again.

Blood splattered onto the tiled floor after I knocked two of her teeth out. I didn't stop even after I realized that I'd knocked her unconscious. Screaming like a maniac, I continued pounding on her face like my mission was to kill her. She damn sure deserved it after trying to murder me.

Yuri didn't know that when I went into my room earlier, I'd fashioned a body armor out of Nyri's old magazines. I had used the tape I'd stolen from the nurse's office to tape the outdated magazines all around my chest and abdomen. I knew that bitch was coming for me so I made sure that she wouldn't catch me slipping—and she almost did, had it not been for me thinking on my feet.

In the distance, I heard Nyri call out for me to stop but I couldn't and I wouldn't. Rage and hatred had completely taken over my body as I bashed Yuri's face in with my fists. I felt her nose break after the fifth punch but I still continued to hit her. By the time I finished with this bitch, she would need reconstructive surgery to correct the damage.

"That's enough, Diana! Chill the fuck out! The C.O.s are coming!" Nyri said, pulling me off of her.

Everyone quickly fled the scene, leaving Yuri unconscious in a puddle of her own blood. Even her girls had abandoned her since they didn't want to be associated with the incident. Being involved in any way was an automatic trip to the SHU.

Nyri and Bianca whisked me away to the cell so that I could wash the blood off my hands. If the guards found out that I was the one fighting, they'd charge me with a felonious assault in addition to more time.

I didn't want those problems.

Bianca quickly turned on the sink for me while Nyri rushed to get something to wrap my hand in. I was trembling uncontrollably as I allowed the warm water to pour over my wounds. To be honest, it could've been worse. Much worse. Apart from a few nicks here and there, I had no real injuries besides the cut on my hand.

When the red alarm sounded off, I knew the C.O.s had finally discovered Yuri's body in the rec room. I had dog-walked that hoe, and there was no doubt she'd be spending a substantial amount of time in the infirmary. At least now that bitch would think twice about fucking with me.

12

ROXIE

The following morning, Kwon showed up on my doorstep with roses and breakfast from my favorite restaurant. He even made a pit stop at the grocery store to grab Rain's favorite apple sauce.

Before he had shown up, I was under the assumption that he'd gone back to Korea without me. And deep down inside, I was happy that he'd stayed. I didn't want to end things on a bad note. We were better than that.

"I'm surprised you still in Atlanta," I said over omelets and skillet potatoes. We decided to eat in the living room since he hadn't set up the dining table yet. "Yesterday you made it seem as if you had something really important to take care of."

"You're more important," he told me.

I blushed and smiled a bit shyly at the handsome young man before me. Kwon always knew what to say and when to say it. "But you're still leaving soon though, right?" I couldn't hide the disappointment in my tone.

Kwon reached over and touched my thigh. "Let's not talk about that. Today, I just wanna enjoy your company," he said. "Allow me to make up for the way I've been acting lately. You know that's not me. Give me a chance. I wanna make you reconsider my proposal."

***

That day, I decided to give myself a much needed break. After calling the sitter, I showered, got dressed, and embarked on a spectacular date with Kwon. Mimosas in a hot air balloon overlooking the city was our first stop, followed by a breathtaking ride on the Ferris wheel in downtown Atlanta. Afterwards, we were picked up in a Maybach Exelero by one of his chauffeurs and dropped off at Lenox Square Mall. Kwon gave me his credit cards to use with no limitations. I bought several designer bags, each valued at more than five grand.

To cap off our wonderful day, he and I enjoyed a relaxing evening of pampering at a luxury spa in midtown. As much as I wanted to stay mad at Kwon, I couldn't be angry with a man who spoiled me with thoughtful gifts and romantic gestures.

By the time our night ended, he had reminded me why I fell in love with him in the first place. Kwon treated me like a queen. He made me feel beautiful and secure in myself— even with the permanent scars on my body.

He was also loyal, never once giving me a reason to feel like there was someone else he treated as special as me. He continued to chase me, even when I was already his. Kwon was good to me and my family, and honestly, I couldn't have asked for a better man. The only thing about him I didn't like was the fact that he kept so many secrets.

When we got back to my house, I found the nanny fast asleep in the rocking chair next to Rain's crib. Tapping her lightly on the shoulder, I woke her up and informed her that we had returned. Kwon was nice enough to tip her $300 before sending her on her way. As I made myself comfortable on the living room sectional, he went to the kitchen and poured us glasses of champagne.

"You still never told me what happened to your head," I called out to him.

"It's not important," he said, entering the room with two wine glasses.

"See. That's why I fall out with your ass. You can never just be real with me. You don't keep secrets from someone you claim to love—"

"Really? We back on this? After the day we just spent together?"

"Yeah, 'cuz all roads lead back to here," I told him. "The fact that you continue to keep shit from me makes it more and more difficult for me to trust you. How can you expect me to spend my life with somebody I can't even trust?"

Kwon released a deep sigh and pinched the bridge of his nose in frustration. He looked like he wanted to say something smart but he held back from doing so. Probably because he didn't want things to further escalate. It was a wise decision too, because no one—and I meant no one—could out argue me.

"What else do you want, Roxie? I've done everything in my power to make shit right between us...but it's obviously not enough for you. What else do you want from me?"

Today, Kwon went all out, but it meant nothing if he couldn't be honest and upfront with me. "I just want the truth! What's so hard about that?"

Kwon was silent.

"Tell me! I need to know 'cuz I don't want shit coming back on me and me baby. Where in the hell are you getting all this gotdamn money?" My patience had finally run thin. Now I was demanding for him to tell me the truth.

"Roxie—"

I quickly cut him off. "Do you sell drugs?"

"No."

"Do you sell stolen cars?"

Kwon grimaced. "No."

"Are you a hit-for-hire?"

"No..."

I had literally named all of my ex's occupations. There was desperation in my eyes when I said, "I need to know where this money is coming from!"

There was a long, drawn out silence before Kwon spoke calmly.

"How 'bout I show you?"

I didn't fully understand what he meant by that but it sounded like progress nonetheless.

"I don't want to hide anything from you anymore. I want everything out in the open," he told me. "Because I see how unhappy this makes you...and I don't want you to be unhappy. If I'm not making you happy then what the fuck am I doing?"

I stared at Kwon with earnest eyes as he spoke to me in a soothing voice.

"I don't want to lose you, Roxie. Not over this." He reached over and massaged the nape of my neck. "I love you."

"I love you too," I whispered, turned on by his gentle touch and seductive gaze.

Before I could agree to his proposition, Kwon was on his knees in front of me, tugging off my skin-tight high waist jeans. Once they were finally off, he pulled me further down on the couch, pushed my panties to the side, and licked my pussy.

"*Mmm.*" A soft whimper broke free after the tip of his tongue glided across my throbbing clit.

Moving it in a brush-stroking pattern, he tickled my bud until my cheeks flushed and toes curled. If pussy eating was an art, Kwon was Picasso.

Grabbing my hands, he placed them on the back of his head, giving me full control of his rhythm. I shivered in ecstasy as he French-kissed my clit, slipping his tongue inside me every so often. Kwon was so gentle and passionate with everything he did. He took his time pleasuring me, savoring the taste of my nectar and paying special attention to my most sensitive areas. When Kwon finally found the spot that made my eyes roll to the back of my head, he continued to lick, flick and suck until I squirted all over his chin.

"*Arrrrrrrggggghhhh!*"

"*Ssh.*" Kwon reached up and softly covered my mouth. "You're gonna wake the baby..." He then slipped two of his fingers in my mouth, which I sucked and swirled my tongue around. I was more than ready for the real thing. Unable to take any more foreplay, I reached for his belt but he stopped me.

"No. Right now it's all about you." Kwon's voice was hoarse as he spoke. "I just wanna please you, baby. Can I do that for you?"

Biting my bottom lip in pleasure, I ran my fingers through his silky, jet black hair. Kwon had both of my legs wide open and his head buried deep in between my thighs. "*Yesss*, baby," I moaned. "Shit...you can do whatever you want to me. I'm yours..."

Kwon must've relished hearing that because he started eating my pussy like it was his last meal. "For how long, Roxie?" He kissed and nibbled on my button in between each word.

"Forever," I breathed.

He was sucking on my clit so good that I forgot why we were even fighting...and within seconds, I came a second time.

"Kwon...!" I cried out in pleasure after he slid two fingers deep inside me.

"*Unh-unh.* I'm not done with you yet," he whispered.

"I...don't think I can cum anymore..."

Kwon pushed his thumb into my asshole. "Let's see..."

Reclining my head, I reveled in the sensation he was creating. Every so often, he would curve his fingers to tickle my G-spot. Kwon knew my body like we'd been lovers for years.

Before I knew it, I came again...this time harder than the last two.

Pulling drenched fingers out, he sucked the wetness off of each one. Damn, this dude was a freak.

"Come here."

Taking me by the hand, Kwon pulled me down onto the white fur rug with him and spread my legs far apart. I was so weak and physically drained but that didn't stop him in his mission at making me cum a fourth time.

Honestly, I didn't think I had another orgasm in me, but apparently I was wrong. Kwon ate my pussy well into the next morning. My muscles ached from cumming so many times. He had literally sucked all of the frustration and doubt out of me. And when he asked if I would accompany him to Korea, I happily agreed without a second thought.

13
MAGYC

"Fuck you been at?"

Michael was on my back the minute I entered our newly remodeled shop. The last one had been torched by Cameron's crazy ass ex-boyfriend, Jag. To ensure that something like that never happened again, I moved the operation to a more secluded location.

Tucked off in the outskirts of Allenhurst, Georgia was an abandoned asylum that we now used as a headquarters for our enterprise. The small town was almost 4 hours from Atlanta and situated near the ocean, making transportation of the stolen vehicles that much easier.

"Damn, my nigga, you questioning me like we fuckin'. Fall back, blood."

A few of the fellas working on the Porsche nearby chuckled. The building was always filled with people either working on cars, changing VIN numbers, or prepping them for shipment. The place was like one big automotive shop with trap music, two bars, plush furniture, and dancers that performed on rotating stages.

I'd dropped some serious coins to have the entire place renovated. Before I came along, it was pretty much condemned with Do Not

Enter signs posted in the front of the building.
Those, I actually chose to leave up.

"It ain't like you to be MIA though,"
Michael said. He was my older brother and the
lieutenant of our organization. He mostly
handled inventory as well as the financial aspect.
He used to be Jude's right hand until he left me in
charge.

Michael pretty much lived at the shop
since he didn't have shit else to do. A couple
years back Jag killed his wife and daughter,
leaving him with nothing but wealth to live for.

"Niggas go missing everyday, B. That's my
business," I told him.

"Yeah...but this car shit is *our* business.
And I can't run this mothafucka by myself."

"I doubt you'd even be capable." The
shade was unnecessary but I didn't appreciate
the way he was coming at me. Michael may've
been my big bro, but I was the nigga who signed
his paychecks.

"Man, wassup wit'chu?" Michael finally
asked. "You been actin' uptight ever since ya old
pussy been under new management."

I almost hit his ass in the mouth over that
comment but I decided to let it slide. "Bruh, chill.
Not today."

Michael shook his head at me in pity.
"Damn. Look at'chu, man. I hate seeing you like

this. You taking it worse than me after I lost my family."

I didn't want to talk about it, so I shrugged him off and lit a blunt. I was supposed to be going over the new inventory list with him but I was too focused on Roxie. What I needed to do was take my mind off of her and accept that it was over so that I could start putting this money on rotation.

Michael was right. I had been slacking lately ever since my break up, abusing my responsibilities as boss. If I didn't get my shit together and soon, our business would fold.

"You need something to help you get over that bitch...'cuz this moping around shit...It's fucking pathetic." Michael pointed to one of the girls on stage. She had the fattest ass out of all of them. Her tits weren't too bad either. "Why don't you take dat ass to the back. Let her get'chu together."

She smiled at me while seductively rubbing her breasts. "I *guarantee* I can get you together, baby."

"So can I," another added. She then stuck her middle finger in the other girl's pussy, ready to get a threesome popping off.

"If you take them, you gotta take me too," a third one piped up.

They all wanted to fuck a boss nigga. And on any other occasion, I would've indulged but right now my heart just wasn't in it. "Nah. I'mma pass."

"*Aww.*" All three girls pouted in unison.

"Damn, boy. How the fuck you turn down three freaky ass bitches? You must be outta yo' mothafucking mind! Lame to the game," he laughed.

I waved him off. "I don't want them bitches, man. You know who the fuck I want."

"Well she done already made it clear she don't want you," Michael said. "It's time to let that bougie bitch go. It's plenty other groupies out here just like her. This ain't even like you to be sweating no panties like this. You weren't even this tight at Briana's funeral. What the fuck is it about this bitch that got yo' balls in a bunch?"

I ignored Michael and his comment about my ex's funeral. Jag had murdered her the same day that he attacked Roxie. Just hearing him mention it made me feel uneasy and brought back so many painful memories I wanted desperately to forget.

I swear this nigga really loves pushing my mothafucking buttons. If I didn't know any better, I'd think he was purposely trying to get a reaction out of me. But all he was going to get was his mothafucking teeth kicked out his mouth.

"Fuck it. I say we pull up to the Flame tonight." Michael rubbed his dry hands together like a nigga would after rolling dice. "That's where you met her, right? We can find a bitch that looks just like her...I'm sure there's plenty." Losing his family had turned him into a bitter, insensitive asshole. Michael didn't even put any thought into the reckless shit that came out his mouth. The nigga had absolutely no chill. "I even think I saw a couple with some scars and bullet wounds—"

Michael's neck snapped back after I punched the shit out of his ass. Making jokes about Roxie's scars was not something I would tolerate. Not from him. Not from anyone. Now he was taking shit too far.

"What the fuck—"

"I don't give a fuck if we together or not! That's still my mothafucking girl! And I ain't gon' tolerate you disrespecting her!"

"How the fuck is she yo' mothafucking girl ridin' 'round with a Chink? You trying to claim some pussy that ain't even yours!"

"That pussy always gon' be mine! And say something else, mothafucka! You gon' be picking yo'self up off the ground, bitch!"

"Damn. I was just fucking wit'chu man," he said, wiping the blood off his chin. His bottom lip was leaking but he didn't get anything he didn't deserve. "Gotdamn. What the fuck is wrong wit'chu? Over a bitch though? You get no stripes for that weak ass shit."

Snatching my pistol out, I pressed the cold steel to his head. "Now you can fuck around again on that bullshit and get two to yo' mothafucking head."

Everyone that was in the room stopped what they were doing to spectate. They all expected the gun to go off at any moment. And it would have too, if it weren't for the simple fact that Michael was my brother.

"Unless you gon' squeeze, you better get that mothafucka out my face," Michael said through clenched teeth.

I gave him a menacing stare. "Mothafucka, don't tempt me."

All of a sudden, I heard a shrill, high-pitched whistling noise followed by a loud, earth-shattering explosion.

BOOM!

The entire building shook violently before the cement ceiling caved in and collapsed on top of us.

14
MAGYC

When I opened my eyes, I was completely engulfed in flames and thick pillars of smoke. Debris and dead bodies surrounded me, and it took a moment to realize the destroyed building was now ablaze.

If I didn't want the fire or falling rubble to kill me, I had to get out of there and fast. As soon as I tried to sit up, a sharp pain shot throughout my entire body. There was a jagged piece of metal lodged deep in my shoulder blade and another in my left leg.

Bracing myself for the pain sure to come, I reached for the fragment and snatched it out of my thigh. When I tried to do the same to the one in my arm, it didn't pull out as easily as the first one.

"*Michael*...!" My voice came out weak and raspy because of my smoke-filled lungs. "Michael!"

I didn't see him anywhere. I was just about to look for him when I noticed the dancers huddled in a corner screaming for their lives. They were surrounded by flames and car wreckage.

Pulling off my Saint Laurent jacket, I placed it over my head for protection and ran through the fire towards them. My arm was burned a little in the process, but because of the adrenaline coursing through my body I didn't feel it.

Once I reached them, I put my jacket over the women and helped lead them out of the ruins. After making sure they'd safely gotten out of the building, I went back inside to find my brother.

By then, the place was so smoked out that it was hard for me to see. Snatching a nearby cloth off the ground, I used it to cover my nose to keep me from inhaling carbon monoxide.

I combed the place, moving chunks of cement out of my path, and helping anyone I found along the way.

"MICHAEL!" I called out his name until my voice went hoarse. With every second that passed, I could feel my body growing weaker and weaker. I was gradually succumbing to the poisonous gas.

Coughing and struggling to see, I climbed through the remains in search of my brother. I finally found him, nearly ten feet from where we were standing before the explosion. He was unconscious with lacerations to his face and chest.

Half-running, half-limping, I rushed to his aid with the sharp piece of metal still protruding from my arm. However, my own injuries were the last thing on my mind.

"Mic..." I coughed, choked, and gagged on the smoke before falling to my knees weakly. Shit. We were both going to die in this bitch. Together.

Dropping to the ground in defeat, I reached over and grabbed Michael's bloody hand. If I'd known that death was imminent, I would've never spent our final moments bickering.

Closing my eyes, I accepted my fate. I was ready to meet my God...

Suddenly, Roxie's face flashed into my mind. I thought about Rain, and being there to see her first steps, and it gave me enough strength to get up off the ground.

Using what little energy I had, I crawled over to Michael and pulled him from underneath the rubble that had fallen on top of him. His right leg was mangled but by the mercy of God, he was still breathing.

I was able to drag him out of the burning building just seconds before it collapsed in flames. Because everyone was in a state of panic, no one noticed the Mercedes pickup truck parked halfway across the field.

There were two people inside the vehicle; a man and a woman. The man was driving and the woman was stationed on the bed of the truck with a rocket-propelled grenade launcher. I couldn't believe that Kwon had the balls to send some killers after me.

Oh, this mothafucka wanna play, huh? It's aight. This mothafucka wanna burn my building down. I'mma burn they whole mothafucking world down. I'm putting prices on all those mothafuckas' heads.

You never underestimate the enemy.

Thinking about the state that my brother was in made me want to kill a mothafucka. *Any and everybody that had something to do with this shit better be trying to protect their family. 'Cuz shit 'bout to go down.*

Reaching for my pistol, I soon realized that I didn't have it. I must've dropped it inside the building after the explosion.

I guess it's just not their time right now...but their time will come.

Because the truck was far away, and it was night time, they couldn't see me but I could see them. They were the same couple who jumped out of Kwon's trunk the day of our confrontation.

Satisfied with the damage they'd caused, they drove off, disappearing into the night as mysteriously as they came. I wanted to tell somebody to follow them but the smoke had rendered me speechless.

Fuck it.

I'll deal with those mothafuckas at a later date.

15
KWON

Staring off into space, I absentmindedly tapped my ballpoint pen against the desk in my hotel room. It was a habit I often did whenever I was anxious or in deep thought. For the last few hours, I'd been on pins and needles waiting for my line to ring with good news.

This whole fucked up situation had my nerves on edge, and without thinking, I snapped the Cuban cigar in half.

Damn. What's taking these assholes so long?

In order to ease my frustration, I poured a generous amount of cognac and downed it straight, no chaser. "I guess if you want something done right, you gotta do it yourself."

I was just about to pour another shot when my business line rang.

Right on time.

Pressing the lime button, I placed the phone against my ear. "This better be good."

"It's done," Kim said in a deep, low voice. I could hear the engine of his truk humming in the background, so I knew he and Sara were still on the road.

"Are you sure?" I asked him. I wanted to be positive before hanging up, because I wouldn't be able to sleep another day while that motherfucker was still alive.

"We saw the entire place go up in smoke and flames. Trust me. No one made it out of there alive."

Pleased with the news, I disconnected the call and tossed back the shot of Cognac in front of me. A celebratory drink was well deserved.

I love it when a plan comes together.

Now that I was determined to make Roxie my wife, I couldn't allow Magyc to come in between us. They say jealousy is love in competition, and I refused to compete with anyone for her heart. Therefore, I eliminated my competition.

Maybe I'll do the honors of paying for his funeral, I thought deviously. *It was the least I could do.*

Now that Magyc was finally out of the picture, Roxie and I could move on.

16

MAGYC

"I'm leveling shit! Them mothafucking Chinks wanna war—I'mma give they mothafucking asses a war! I'm putting numbers on all them dog-eating bitches—and anybody that looks like 'em!" In a fit of rage, I punched the wall in the hospital's hallway. I was so pissed off that I could've easily killed someone just for looking at me the wrong way. "My mothafucking brother in the operating room! They gotta cut his fucking leg off! Man, this shit ain't even fucking real!"

Pulling on my own dreads, I felt as if I were going crazy. Like I was stuck in a bad dream that I couldn't wake up from. This shit was not happening.

"Tell me how you wanna handle this shit," Asher said.

He was my third in command after Michael and also the muscle of my operation. Any problems I had, Asher went to see about it. The nigga had more bodies than a morgue. And right now, I needed killers like that on my team because as much as I hated to admit it, I had underestimated Kwon.

"I need history on all them mothafuckas," I said, wiping the spit off my chin. I was so angry and riled up that I was foaming at the mouth.

Knowing that my brother was being operated on as we spoke fucked me up. Somebody had to die over this shit, somebody had to mothafucking pay. And I wouldn't stop combing the streets until that mothafucka was dealt with.

***

When I got back to the crib later on that night, the first person that I called was Roxie. After everything that'd happened, I didn't want to be alone. But I didn't want just anyone's company either. It was a quarter after 3 a.m. when I banged her line but she still picked up.

"What do you want, Magyc?" she asked in a groggy tone.

"I'm sorry...I just couldn't make another move without hearing your voice."

"Well, you've heard it. I'm going back to sleep now—"

"Hold up. Damn. You just gon' hang up on me?"

"Have you been drinking again?" she asked. "Why are you calling me so early in the morning anyway?"

"Can you come through? Or can I pull up on you?"

Roxie sighed deeply, not answering me immediately. She was apprehensive about inviting me over only because she didn't want me to have another run in with her lil' boyfriend.

In the back of my mind, that was just what I was hoping for.

The next time I see that nigga it's on sight.

"Magyc, you and I both know that ain't a good idea," she said.

I wanted to let her know that I'd almost gotten killed...that my brother had to lose a leg. I wanted to tell her everything...but I didn't.

"I need you," were the words that fell out of my mouth instead.

"Call Tara," she said matter-of-factly.

"Man, fuck Tara...I'm on the phone with my woman."

"Not for long. Goodbye, Magyc—"

"Wait. Don't hang up..." I pleaded. "Look, I don't want shit from you, aight. I ain't trying to beat your back out. I just wanna talk. That's all." Releasing a deep breath, I raked my fingers through my golden mid-length dreadlocks. "I really could use a legit voice of reasoning. And right now I can't talk to my brother...or the niggas on my payroll. And you're the only person I trust enough to see me like this..."

If my boys saw me feeble and mentally debilitated they'd begin to question my capabilities as leader and I couldn't have that shit. Especially during crucial times like this.

There was a long pause on Roxie's end. I could tell she was thinking hard about it. Mulling over the idea of seeing me again after everything I'd put her through. She must've heard the desperation in my tone because surprisingly she agreed.

"I have a flight to catch in a few hours. So I can't stay long."

***

It was half past five when I heard a faint knock at my front door. I'd accidentally dozed off on the couch waiting for Roxie to show up...and for a second I had forgotten that I invited her over.

On instinct, I grabbed the loaded 9 off the glass coffee table in front of me. Underneath the sofa was a AR SKS with the extended banana clip. Fucking around with me, somebody was gonna catch a bullet.

Standing to my feet, I walked sluggishly to the front of my loft. I finally relaxed after looking through the peephole and seeing that it was Roxie on the other end. Tucking the gun in the waist of my jeans, I typed in the code to my electronic deadbolt.

My entire body was sore from the injuries I'd sustained, but I still mustered up enough strength to answer the door with a smile and firm embrace. I was happy as hell that she climbed out of bed at the crack of dawn just to see me.

Perhaps there was still a possibility that

she loved me...Or perhaps she was just being thoughtful. Maybe she even pitied me. Either way, I appreciated her presence.

Roxie barely let me hold her for two seconds before pulling away. "I came to lend an ear. Not to be groped on."

Damn. She always knew how to kill a mothafucking mood.

"I was only hugging you."

"I don't know where the fuck your hands been lately."

Her pettiness actually made me laugh, and I was surprised that I could after everything that happened today.

"Last I checked, you can talk without touching," she said in a sassy tone.

"Aight then." I smiled. "I'll try to keep my hands to myself." My eyes roamed over her body, and the way her ass sat up in the Hello Kitty pajama pants she wore.

Roxie plopped into an empty barstool and folded her arms. "The nanny was pissed about me getting her out of bed this early."

"Let her know I owe her one," I said. "And where you supposed to be flying to anyway?"

"Overseas."

"Overseas where."

Roxie looked unamused. "Magyc, you've

got five minutes."

"Damn. That's all I'm worth?"

"Three minutes."

"I fucked up, Rox!" I blurted out. "I fucked bad."

Roxie looked confused. "Magyc, what are you—" Suddenly, her gaze shifted to my shoulder. "Shit, Magyc—you're bleeding!"

When I looked down, I saw that blood was soaking through my t-shirt. I must've torn the stitches and not realized it.

Rushing to the bathroom, she grabbed a wet washcloth and bandages out of the medicine cabinet. When she entered the living room again, I was struggling to pull off the shirt with my fucked up arm.

"What the fuck, Magyc? I swear to God it's always something with you. What type of messy ass trouble have you gotten yourself into now?" she asked, dabbing at my wound.

I winced a little because she was being rough. "What makes you think I'm the one starting the trouble?"

"Convince me otherwise."

"I didn't call you here to convince you of anything."

"Well, why did you call me? Is there something you wanna tell me?"

"Like what?"

"Like what happened to you. Who did this?" Roxie asked, staring at the burns on my left forearm.

"Doesn't matter. They'll be dealt with soon enough."

Roxie sighed in frustration. "Magyc...I'm lost..."

I wasn't surprised. I was talking in circles.

"What happened?" she asked again, this time in a much gentler tone. "Magyc...? Talk to me."

I had totally spaced out as I stared at the electric fireplace in front of us. I could still smell smoke and burning flesh. Coming so close to death had thrown me all off. Not to mention, the financial loss.

Kwon had destroyed over half a million dollars' worth of merchandise. In addition to starting over from scratch, I had to hope and pray my soldiers stayed committed to the cause.

We'd had too many fatal incidents within the last two years, and that wasn't a good look for our business. For the clients, it'd be too big of a liability, and for the workers, it'd be too much of a risk. I couldn't lose customers and I couldn't have niggas jumping ship. I had to ensure the safety of my business as well as the lives of my men. I needed everything to pan out because I had to make this shit work. I couldn't go back to being a stick up kid. That shit was over with.

"Magyc...?"

My grim thoughts were disrupted by Roxie's calming tone.

When I looked up into her eyes, I clearly saw that she still cared about me. Suddenly, and without thinking, I leaned in and kissed her.

17
MAGYC

In the beginning, Roxie tried to put up a fight, and it was obvious she was battling some internal feelings. However, all of her struggles seemed to dissolve the moment that my hands went to her waist. Gently latching onto her midsection, I carefully eased her into my lap. It had been months since I held her in this way and I'd actually forgotten what she felt like.

When I slipped my tongue between her lips, Roxie quickly drew back. "Magyc...wait...we shouldn't," she whispered.

I wasn't trying to listen to that shit though. The only thing I wanted to hear was her chanting for me to go faster, deeper, and harder. My dick instantly sprang to life at the mere thought. I had to have her sexy ass and I wasn't taking no for an answer.

Ignoring her pleas for me to stop, I tugged on her shirt and pulled her even closer to me. Her mouth said no but her eyes screamed fuck me. She wanted me just as badly as I wanted her.

Within seconds, Roxie was on top of me in a straddling position, rocking against the erection bulging through my jeans. Damn. She had me harder than a bitch. So hard that I was ready to go in balls deep without protection.

"*Mmm...*" A low, animalistic groan escaped me as I squeezed on her plush ass. I loved that she was natural. No surgery, no shots. All organic, just how I liked my bitches.

Sliding my hands inside her pants, I squeezed on her bare ass so hard that she cringed a little. Oftentimes, I'd been told that I was a tad bit aggressive. Maybe too aggressive.

In attempt to calm me down enough to think rationally, she placed her hands against my chest. "Magyc...we can't..." Roxie said.

Grabbing her by the wrists, I yanked her back towards me and kissed her again, sucking and nibbling on her pillowy soft lips.

"Don't tell me what I can't do..." I demanded, my voice hoarse with lust.

My mouth lefts hers and traveled down towards her neck, causing soft moans to fill the room. I'd familiarized myself with every sensitive area on her body. I knew every spot that got her going. Knew her body better than I knew my own.

"Ma...gyc..." Her voice broke up after I slipped my hand down the front of her pants.

We should've stuck to keeping a safe distance from each other. Now it was too late.

"Didn't nobody tell you...you could give my pussy away."

I talked big shit in Roxie's ear as I stroked

her kitty with my fingers. She was so mothafucking wet for someone who was intent on not having sex.

"If you'd acted right, I wouldn't have had to," she whispered.

Hearing her say that shit made me bite her chin. "Don't fucking play with me." I then tugged on her top. "Matter fact...take this shit off."

Surprisingly, Roxie complied without any lip. Next, her pants came off followed by her boy shorts. My mouth watered at the sight of her shaved pussy. That mothafucka was fat, pretty and glistening with her juices.

"Pull my dick out." My voice was barely above a whisper.

Roxie reached for my Hermes belt but paused midway. "You know we shouldn't be doing this," she said apprehensively.

I looked her dead in the eyes and said, "If you really believed that, you wouldn't even be here."

Roxie couldn't help but smile at my straightforwardness. I was only speaking facts.

Biting her bottom lip seductively, she reached for my belt and carefully unbuckled it. After pulling out ten inches of steel, she gently stroked it in her tiny hand.

"Climb up on it..."

Roxie hesitated, almost as if she were struggling with the decision on whether to do so or not. Ultimately, she decided to hop on board.

"Shit," I breathed after she slid down on top of my dick. She was so warm, so wet, so tight. Damn. It had been too long since I felt this pussy. Too long.

Thrusting my hips underneath her weight, I gave her every inch of me. And judging from the way she was bucked, moaned, and screamed, I could tell her nigga wasn't hitting it right.

"He be fucking you like this?" I asked her.

Her pussy was wet and gripping my dick like she never wanted me to leave.

Grabbing one of her breasts, I popped a rigid nipple into my mouth. "Nah. He don't be fucking you like this."

Wrapping one arm around my neck, Roxie rode me faster. She was like a horse jockey on a stallion, bouncing to the rhythm of our pace. With her free hand, she interlocked her fingers in mine and kissed me like she meant forever.

"Shit, Magyc...I'm 'bout to cum!"

"Go 'head. Cum on this dick, baby. Cum on it..."

I coached her until she finally convulsed with her first orgasm while crying out how much she loved me.

I kissed her collarbone and the side of her neck. "Was it as good to you as it was to me, baby?"

"Yes, baby."

"You still love me?"

Suddenly, regret flashed across her face. Climbing off of me, she quickly grabbed her clothes off the floor and redressed. She was just about to pull her shirt on when I grabbed her wrist and jerked her back onto my lap.

"Where the fuck you think you going? Back to that Chink?"

"My whereabouts is not your concern."

"Any and everything you do is always my concern."

Roxie stood to her feet to leave. "Magyc, I gotta go."

"How well you know that mothafucka?" I asked. I was no saint, but at least with me she knew what she was getting.

"Well enough to know he makes me feel good, inside and out."

"Is *that* right...?"

There was a long pause between us.

"Oh, okay..."

"Is that all of your questions?"

"You trust him well enough to take my

baby out the country with him?"

"How many times I gotta tell you. Rain is not your daughter. Therefore, you have no say so in what I do with my child—"

"I wish you'd stop saying that shit."

Roxie tossed her hands up and copped an attitude. "You know what? I don't have time for this shit. I've only got a few hours to pack and get ready—"

"Man, you ain't going no mothafucking where with that nigga! You barely even know that mothafucka!"

"Yeah, and I barely know you! You did some fucked up shit to me, Magyc, that I never even thought you were capable of. You've lied to me! You've kept secrets from me—a whole fucking child! And speaking of which, how's he doing? Have you been to see him lately?"

I immediately fell silent because I hadn't.

"You need to focus on your own life before trying to dictate mine." And with that, she headed towards the front door.

"Roxie!" I quickly stopped her just seconds before she walked out.

Roxie stopped and turned to face me. "What?" she snapped.

"Stay the fuck away from that nigga."

"...Why?"

"'Cuz that mothafucka ain't who you think he is."

18
ROXIE

Despite Magyc's warning, I still flew to Seoul with Kwon in a beautiful, luxury private business jet. After a grueling 14-hour flight, we were picked up by his driver in an $800,000 Hongqi L5. Up until then, I had never set eyes on the luxury Chinese car. And the fact that he was even able to afford one only made me more curious about what he did for a living.

Kwon did however promise to tell me now that I was in Korea with him, and now it was simply a matter of when. In the meantime, I would enjoy the beautiful metropolitan city and all of its hidden treasures.

During the flight, Kwon told me all about the tourist attractions, shopping malls, and temples throughout Seoul, and I couldn't wait to go exploring. Just being in Korea felt like a vacation that was much needed. It was breathtaking and unique, in a way that was both welcoming and refreshing. I felt like I was in another world and I was excited to indulge myself in the city's culture.

Staring out of the window at the passing scenery, I was like a kid in Disneyland during the ride to his home. My jaw literally dropped the moment we pulled into a gated mansion overlooking the mountains.

"*This* is where you live? *Here?*" I tried my best to mask the excitement in my tone. I knew that Kwon was racked up, but I had no idea to what extent. His place was as big as Buckingham Palace and just as opulent.

"On occasion," he said. "But I own multiple properties throughout Seoul. This one just so happens to be my favorite."

I understood why. It was beyond impressive and tucked off from the rest of society with huge statues and fountains out front. I had never seen a more beautiful residence.

After parking, the driver unloaded our suitcases and we climbed out and walked towards the house together. Two young women and a maid were waiting for us at the door. I couldn't help but notice they all were avoiding eye contact with me.

Damn. What gives, I thought to myself.

"Seokwon!" the youngest of the women cried out. She then ran up to him and flung her arms around his neck.

For his sake, I hope she's related to him.

Unfortunately, I didn't find out immediately since they started speaking to each other in Korean. Shortly after, the other woman joined in, greeting him with a similarly affectionate hug. The maid respectively hung back.

For several seconds, I simply stood there with Roxie's car seat in my hand while they talked about only God knows what. Neither woman even made an effort to greet me or acknowledge the small child I was carrying— which in my opinion was pretty rude. In an effort to make my presence known, I cleared my throat to remind Kwon that I was still here.

"My apologies, love." Kwon took me by the hand and pulled me closer to him. "I would like to introduce you to my sisters. Well...two of 'em at least. This here is Hae-Won," he said, pointing to the tallest. She was slender with brunette hair and a cherubic face. The shorter, spunkier one had heavy eyeliner and strawberry blond hair. "And the red head is Sun."

I waved at them both even though they seem unenthused by my presence.

What a couple of standoffish bitches.

They looked so nice and wholesome in the pictures Kwon had shown me but in real life they seemed to be the exact opposite. With their unfriendly attitudes and half-assed greetings, I got the immediate feeling that they didn't want me here.

"Hae-Won and Sun...this is Roxie. My fiancé."

I quickly cut my eyes at him after introducing me as his soon-to-be wife. I hadn't even accepted his proposal and he was already telling his folks that we were getting married.

Hae-Won and Sun looked just as surprised as me. Kwon had shocked all of us. Hae-Won said something in Korean to which Kwon dismissively waved off. Defeated, she and Sun went back into the house with no further words left to exchange.

Once they were completely out of earshot, I turned to Kwon. "Why did you tell them I was your fiancé?"

Kwon's eyes twinkled with amusement. "You're not?"

"Kwon...I still don't know if I wanna go through with this—"

"Don't worry," he said, taking my hands in his. "I'm sure I'll change your mind."

***

The following morning, I was surprised with a hearty full course meal in bed. When I was asleep, Kwon had an entire catering team stop by to prepare grilled short ribs, spicy seafood salad, beansprout rice, stewed fish, and cucumber soup. It was one of the most romantic things a man had ever done for me and I was touched.

Shaking my head, I smiled at Kwon as he watched me from the doorway. "You did not have to do all this for me."

"Nonsense," he said. "You deserve to be treated this way everyday."

His comment made me blush. "So what are our plans for the day? Will we be spending it together? Have you handled that business you spoke of?"

"Later," he simply said. "After you eat, I want you to get dressed. There's something I wanna show you."

A big grin spread across my face. I just knew that I was in for another surprise. "Okay."

After a long, hot shower, I slipped into a white maxi dress and blue Versace sandals. By the time I was ready, Kwon was outside waiting for me in a matte black Aventador with the spoiler kit. His cars were just as lavish back home as they were in the states. Suddenly, finding out what he did for a living wasn't as important. I simply wanted to bask in all of the luxury. He had me feeling like I was a queen.

The ride to where ever Kwon was taking me lasted an hour and a half. And by the time we finally arrived at a remote warehouse, I had a look of confusion on my face. "What is this? Why are we here?"

Kwon turned off the engine. "You'll see soon enough." He then climbed out of the car and walked over to the passenger side. Opening the door, he held his hand out for me to take.

For several seconds, I simply stared at it. I had a strange feeling about being there but I shook it off and took his hand anyway. Holding my dress up so that I didn't step on it, I followed him towards the building. After inputting an access code, the doors slid open and we walked inside, and to my surprise the warehouse was empty.

"There's nothing here," I said, looking around. "Why did you bring me here?"

Kwon walked over to a wall-mounted button. "You wanted to know what I do for a living. Well, now you're about to find out."

Suddenly, I began to feel nervous and uncomfortable. My palms were sweating and my heart was beating at a rapid pace. I didn't know what to expect...but I knew that I would finally get the answer to my questions.

"You seem uneasy," Kwon noted. "Are you sure you want this?"

I paused to carefully consider what he was asking. For months, I'd been demanding to know the truth and now that I was this close to finding out, I wasn't certain that I wanted to.

"We don't have to do this if you don't want to," he said. "We *could* just leave here, pretend we never came. Carry on with our lives...with no more questions in regards to what I do. We could just be happy..."

I took a deep, shuddering breath. "Well...we came too far to turn back now."

19
ROXIE

"As you wish." Kwon pushed the button and an aluminum floor door opened up, leading to a staircase.

I stared at it for a while, wondering if I should descend them or not. *Am I really sure I wanna do this?*

"After you," Kwon insisted.

Shaking off my nervousness, I walked towards the door and climbed down the stairs. Luckily, I wasn't wearing any heels, because if I had been, I probably would've bust my ass. Kwon descended the stairs shortly after.

Taking me by the hand, he led me through a white, sterile hall towards a set of steel doors. Beside them was a touch pad that only permitted entry through a fingerprint scanner. After touching his hand against it, the doors slid open, revealing a huge underground factory with high tech equipment and workers in blue scrubs and stocking caps.

What the fuck is this? Some type of hospital?

An icy breeze greeted my skin, causing goose bumps to form all over. I felt like I had just walked into a cooler. *Damn. Why is it freezing cold in here?*

I hesitated to go any further. Something just didn't feel right about being here. Despite my apprehensiveness, Kwon tugged me along anyway. On each side of the room were large glass windows with workers inside, performing some type of...surgical procedure. It was so cold in the factory that the windows had frost build up in the corners.

What is this place, I wondered?

None of what I was seeing made sense to me.

Taking my time, I cautiously walked over to the nearest window. Inside the room, an operation was currently underway. The surgeon's scrubs were stained with blood, pieces of skin, tissue, pus and bodily liquids. Bile quickly shot up my throat but I swallowed it down, nearly gagging on the bitter taste.

"Has your curiosity been fulfilled?" Kwon asked.

When I looked at the cold, lifeless body lying on the metal table, my heart dropped into the pit of my stomach. All of the organs were being removed from a small boy's body. He was so pale as he laid there with his chest cavity wide open. He had to have been at least nine or ten years old.

"What the fuck are ya'll doing in here?" I asked, horrified. "What is this? ...Organ trafficking?!"

"Indeed."

Suddenly, I felt nauseous and lightheaded. Looking around, I realized that everyone in the rooms were being disemboweled, and their organs prepped.

Oh my God. What have I just walked into?

Grabbing the wall, I struggled to keep from fainting. The gruesome sight before me was enough to make me start hyperventilating. I couldn't breathe. I could barely stand on my own two feet. This was just too much.

"What the fuck are you thinking?! THESE ARE HUMAN BEINGS! This shit ain't right!"

Kwon tried to calm me down but I slapped his hand away.

"Get your fucking hands off me!" I screamed. "Don't fucking touch me!"

"See. This is why I didn't wanna let you in on what I had going on—"

"WELL, WHY DID YOU?!"

"Because you insisted on knowing."

"This isn't what I expected!"

The glass must've been sound proof, because the surgeon continued what he was doing without disruption. Tears filled my eyes when I looked at the metal table a second time.

"Why the hell did you bring me here?" I cried softly.

"Just trust me. I've been doing this for years and it's never affected me or anyone around," he said. "I love you, Roxie. I don't wanna have to hide anything from you or keep secrets. You're the woman I wanna spend the rest of my life with."

I quickly tore my gaze away from the window. I couldn't stand to look at the horrendous sight before me another second.

"Believe it or not, you're looking at a forty-four billion dollar industry."

"Well, all money ain't good money. And I don't want anything to do with this! Now get me the fuck out of here!"

"Come on. Let's go. We can talk about this in my office." Kwon tried to pull me towards a door nearby but I pushed him away. I didn't want to talk. I didn't want to be touched. I didn't even want to look at his ass. Just the sight of him disgusted me. Only a sick, soulless person could do some shit like this.

Kwon immediately got frustrated. "You wanted the truth, and I gave you just that."

I shook my head vehemently, clearly in denial of what I was seeing. Organ trafficking was as low as one could go. "Kwon...this...this is inhumane! You're murdering people! What the fuck is wrong with you?! What the fuck are you thinking?! THIS IS SICK AND DEMENTED! That's a child on that table! A little boy! What type of person are you?!"

Kwon reached for my arm but I backed away in terror. I felt like I didn't even know him. Who was this man that was capable of such heinous acts? Magyc tried to warn me and he was so right. Kwon really wasn't who I thought he was.

He was a fucking monster.

Consumed with fear, I took off running for the exit doors. "Let me out of here!" I screamed, banging on the surface.

Kwon calmly walked over towards me, and I had never been more afraid of him in my life. Did he bring me here to kill and harvest my organs too?

I wasn't trying to find out as I pounded on the doors and cried for help. "Somebody let me the fuck out of here!"

"I'mma need you to calm down and get yourself together. I would never hurt you, Roxie."

Ignoring him, I continued to holler at the top of my lungs. "LET ME THE FUCK OUT OF HERE!"

Kwon raised his hand—and I assumed it was to silence me, but instead he reached for the fingerprint scanner. After the doors slid open, I tore off running through the hall and towards the staircase.

I nearly tripped on my way up. I couldn't

get out of that mothafucka fast enough. I was literally sick to my stomach and I needed fresh air desperately. When I reached the steel double doors that led outside, I banged on them frantically as though that would make them automatically open.

When they finally did, I ran outside and threw up everything in my stomach. I could no longer hold it in. The shit that I saw downstairs would haunt me for the rest of my life.

What the fuck was I thinking coming here, I asked myself over and over again. *What the fuck was I thinking ever trusting him?*

He was the same type of man that fleshy part of me always craved. A liar and a criminal. *What is it about me that attracts these crazy ass mothafuckas?*

Kwon walked up and handed me a handkerchief to wipe my mouth. Instead of taking it, I slapped his hand away. I wanted nothing to do with him. "I want you to take me the fuck away from this place! I've seen enough!"

***

"Am I next?" I asked him on the drive back home.

Kwon took his eyes off the road to look at me. "Why would you ask me that?"

"Because I don't wanna end up like those people back there. On a table with my body cut up." Tears poured down my cheeks. I hadn't stopped crying since we left. I cried for all of the victims, especially the little boy whose picture was on a missing poster twenty or so miles outside the city. "I promise I won't say anything. I didn't see anything."

Kwon looked at me like I was crazy. "Roxie...I would never *ever* hurt you. Nothing about me has changed. I'm still the person you fell in love with," he said in a calm voice, like nothing he did was wrong.

"After seeing all that, I'm not so sure I feel the same."

"Don't say that, Roxie." Kwon reached over to touched me and I flinched in fear. "I can't believe you, Rox? You actually think I would harm you?"

I looked at him suspiciously. I didn't know what he was capable of. After seeing all that, I began to wonder if Kwon had anything to do with Magyc getting injured.

All of a sudden, his phone started ringing, breaking up the heavy tension in the car. I listened as Kwon answered and started speaking in Korean. I hated that I couldn't understand a word that he was saying. For all I know, he could've been telling one of the workers to get a room prepared for me.

I was left hanging on the edge of suspense until Kwon finally disconnected the call. When he didn't say anything immediately I decided to speak up. "Please…I just wanna go home…"

"We are going home."

"I…I meant back to America…"

Kwon didn't bat an eyelash when he said, "This is your home now."

20
KWON

After dropping Roxie off, I headed to the Seoul Metropolitan Police Agency to meet with the chief of police. The agency was harboring a witness who was threating to shut down my entire operation. A young woman visiting Seoul on a work visa had been kidnapped by my people, but somehow she managed escaped before they could get her to the factory. When she got to the police department, she told them everything thus putting me and my business in an uncomfortable position. And because of that, I was not happy.

Luckily, me and the chief of police had history. A little persuasion could go a long way and I was determined to make him see things from my angle. So I walked in there with my game face on a three designer piece suit tailored to perfection.

Captain Joo-Won was waiting for me outside of his office the moment I walked in. After a firm handshake, he led me inside, closed the door and ushered for me to take a seat.

"We have an unfortunate situation on our hands," he said in Korean.

"We wouldn't if you'd handled it."

"I wouldn't have to handle anything had

you been more careful," he shot back. "How could you let something like this happen? Your father was never this reckless."

"Well, my father's no longer around," I reminded. "I'm running things now."

Joo-Won raised an eyebrow. "*Are* you?"

I didn't appreciate his tone. "Need I remind you that if this gets out to the public, it could potentially have a devastating impact on your...reputation. This not only affects me. It affects all of us." I then leaned in closer and whispered, "Besides, you owe me one. Let's not forget I'm the reason your son is still alive." A few years back, his son was in need of a heart transplant that he couldn't afford. Thanks to me, I made it possible.

Joo-Won quickly checked his attitude. "What do you need from me?" he asked, in a politer tone.

"Simple. Make the witness and evidence disappear."

"That's not so simple," he said.

"Nonsense. I'm confident that you'll make something happen. And soon," I added.

After our meeting ended, I left out of the headquarters and climbed into my Aventador parked along the street. Revving up the engine, I peeled off, feeling like a burden had been lifted off my chest. Now there was only one more thing to take care of.

Rolling down my window, I tossed Roxie's iPhone in the middle of the street where a truck ran it over. I had taken it prior to dropping her off because I didn't trust her not to call anyone. Any and everybody she wanted to talk to she had to go through me.

If she thinks she's going to get away from me she's out of her motherfucking mind. There's going to be a wedding whether she wants one or not.

21

DIANA

Nyri and I were laughing, talking shit, and lounging when the door to our cell opened. Mr. Asante stepped into the room with a pair of handcuffs dangling by his side. I immediately assumed that he was getting ready to escort me to the security housing unit.

Was this because of my fight with Yuri?

"What's going on?" Nyri asked, jumping off of her bunk.

"Inmate, Prince, let's go."

Although I was confused, I complied with his request nonetheless. Climbing off the top bunk, I turned around and placed my hands behind my back. A second officer stepped inside with a burlap sack and started tossing all of my possessions inside.

"Where are you taking her?" Nyri cried.

"What the fuck did I do?" I asked him.

"Apparently, something right. You're being released."

I burst out crying tears of joy at the unexpected news. *Was he for real? Was I really getting out?* I started to pinch myself until I remembered that I was handcuffed. I didn't trip because I knew that it was only standard protocol.

Nyri quickly ran up to me and hugged me very tight. "Why didn't you tell me?"

"I—I didn't know. If I knew I was getting out today, I would've—"

"It doesn't matter. I'm happy for you," she said, wiping her tears. She smiled and hugged me again. She was the closest thing I had to a sister and I would miss her tremendously. "Remember to slay, pray, and stay out the way," she laughed.

I laughed too. "I will."

"I love you, D."

"I love you too. Take care of yourself."

"Will do. See you on the outs."

After saying our goodbyes, Mr. Asante led me to outtake and past the infirmary where Yuri was being kept. When she saw me walk by, she jumped off the bed and started banging on the glass window. Luckily, she was locked inside.

"Bitch, don't think it's over with! I'mma kill yo' mothafucking ass! When I get out of this mothafucka, bitch you dead! You hear me?! YOU DEAD!" Yuri chucked a glob of spit on the window at me. "I'M GONNA FUCKING MURDER YOU! Just like you did my nephew, bitch! You gon' pay!"

"Just ignore her," Mr. Asante said.

I stuck my middle finger up at her on the

sly and sashayed my ass right down the hall behind him. During processing, I was given my old clothes from the day that I was arrested, and a mandatory $50 to get me where ever I needed to go. I felt like I was dreaming. And if I was, I didn't want to wake up.

"I can't believe I'm actually getting out of here," I said to Mr. Asante as he led me to the exit doors. "This doesn't even feel real."

"Stay your ass out of trouble," he said. "I don't wanna see your ass back here again. You hear me? You understand what I'm saying. I mean that now. I don't wanna see you back here." He then pushed a button that opened up two tall metal gates that led to freedom.

Taking in a deep breath of fresh air, I stepped outside and savored the sweet taste of independence. A year and a half felt like an entire lifetime. I didn't know how I ever thought I'd last 30 years.

When I turned around to thank Mr. Asante for all he had done, he was already gone. All I had to my name was my belongings and fifty measly dollars. Digging in my back pocket, I pulled out the card for the taxi service they had recommended. The money was enough to at least get me to the nearest motel where I could properly shower and get a good night's rest. After that, I would figure out what the hell I was going to do with my life.

At least I ain't gotta go to some crusty ass

halfway house.

I was just about to call the number when a shiny black coupe pulled up on me with extremely dark tinted windows and 26 inch rims. I tried looking inside but it was very hard to see.

Who is this, I thought to myself.

The driver rolled his window down and to my surprise it was Rico. He was wearing Bvlgari sunglasses and a huge Cheshire grin. The diamonds in his grill sparkled like water. ScHoolboy Q's "*Groovy Tony*" poured through the custom speakers.

"Welcome home, baby girl," he said. "You gon' get in or you just gon' stand there looking amazing?"

"I'd rather walk," I told him.

Rico chuckled. "That's the thanks you give Daddy after getting you out?"

"You only cleaned up the mess *you* made."

"Since I cleaned up the mess, don't you think I deserve a reward?"

"People only get rewards when they do good things. Do you honestly think putting me in prison was a good thing?"

"Get in the car. We can talk about it."

"Nah. The walk will do me good."

After a quarter of a mile, I realized that I did want the details about how he had gotten me out. Surprisingly, Rico was still driving beside me at a slow pace, hoping that I'd eventually change my mind about the ride. Against my better judgment, I hopped inside the luxury coupe.

***

On the ride back to the city, Rico told me that he lived in Miami now because Atlanta had gotten too hot for him. From there, he hired a high profile legal team and partnered up with organizations to work on my pardon. He explained how he had the girls revise their statements and admit to giving false confessions. For their crimes, they were each sentenced to community service.

Rico's lawyers were able to produce new evidence that demonstrated my innocence. They also were able to prove that it wasn't my DNA on the murder weapon used to kill Wayne. I assumed Rico had something to do with that. The man was well-connected and known for making shit happen. Because of the time served, the judge dropped all charges on me.

Compensation was promised to me for my troubles, but I wouldn't see that money for a couple of years. To celebrate the good news, Rico treated me to lunch at a popular soul food restaurant in Buckhead. It had been so long since I had a decent meal that I damn near ordered everything on the menu. Cajun pasta, fried calamari, chicken and waffles, and shrimp and grits covered our table, literally taking up every inch of space.

I didn't give a damn about my figure or looking like a pig as I shoved the contents down my throat. When some of the food landed in my lap, I didn't even bother picking it off. I was just that hungry. In prison, I had lost about fifteen pounds because the scrap they served was so disgusting. Now that I was free, I couldn't help but to indulge.

"Damn girl. Slow down," Rico laughed. "That food ain't going nowhere."

"That's why I'm eating it fast. Making sure it don't leave this mothafucking plate."

Rico laughed even harder. "Save some of that energy for me. Don't burn it all out on that plate."

I was just about to say something smart when the waitress walked up to our table. "Can I get you two anything else?" she asked.

"Just the bill," Rico told her.

"Any to-go boxes?"

Rico shook his head. He hated eating food that wasn't fresh.

His fat ass.

"Alright then. I'll be right back with the check."

Rico stood to his feet after she left. "I'mma run to the bathroom real quick."

"Okay…"

After he walked off, I noticed that he'd left his Louis Vuitton wallet and car keys on the table. Reaching over, I grabbed his wallet and opened it to see what he had inside. There were a few credit cards and $700 in cash. Pocketing the money, I grabbed his car keys, slid out of the booth and left the restaurant before he returned.

Now this bitch gon' see how it feels to get left in the mothafucking cold.

22

DIANA

TWO MONTHS LATER

Thinkin' about them licks I hit, I had to...

Thinkin' about if you was here, I had you...

Gon' roll it up my nigga...

Roll up, jump out the car, squeeze the trigger...

Gon' roll it up my nigga...

Roll up, hop out the car, squeeze the trigger...

Future's "*Perkys Calling*" poured through the subwoofers in Persuasion's Gentlemen's Club. My old stomping grounds. After being released from prison, I found myself right back where I'd started. Up on the pole.

It wasn't like I had any other options. I had no diploma, no experience, and I was an ex felon. I had no other choice but to go to back dancing, but ask me if I was complaining. I made $5,000 a week because of my popularity in the Atlanta nightlife, and lived in a beautiful corner unit condo downtown. In addition to Rico's Brabus Coupe, I pushed a white BMW M6 on the weekends. I was living good. Without him.

That night, Persuasion's was packed with so many people that I had to squeeze through just to get around. 50 Cent and Jeezy were in the club that night so everybody that was anybody was up in there.

There was so much money that had been thrown around that there wasn't a single spot on the floor that wasn't covered in dollar bills. I had already made two grand and that was just from working the floor. I hadn't even hit the stage yet, but I knew that when I did I was gonna clean house.

Damn. This bitch rocking.

One section in particular was more lit than the others, crammed with dancers and niggas that looked like rappers or drug dealers. Bottles, blunts, and hookah were being passed around. The niggas had zip loc bags of money filled with stacks and were tossing that shit like it grew on trees.

I frowned my nose up when I saw that there was nothing but basic bitches in their VIP. Oh hell no. *I need to be over there.*

I squeezed through a bunch of broke ass groupie niggas trying to feel my ass. They weren't spending any money and were only there because the celebrities were.

I quickly made my way over to the section—but I stopped as soon as I recognized one of the men.

It was Mr. Asante...and he was conversing with the ringleader of the crew, like he was that nigga in the streets. The guy he was talking to was a regular who occasionally came through with his boys to spend money on Dynasty. I knew him only as Quest.

I didn't know what he did for a living. But I knew that it was probably something illegal because last week one of the men in his crew beat up the club's photographer for trying to take their pics. Those niggas were trouble and I had a feeling that they were into some pretty heavy shit.

I wonder why he's over there talking to them.

Before getting locked up, I'd always danced at Persuasion's and I had never once seen him here.

I'm payin' all my tithes, receivin' bad news...

Lord forgive me for my sins, I know this cash rules...

Future sang his drug anthem as I made my way over towards Mr. Asante. He was deep in conversation and didn't see me walking up. Before I could reach him, some thirsty ass dancer stepped right in his face.

I couldn't stand that bitch or her fucked up ass boob job. The surgical scars had left permanent dents under her nipples and she needed to get that shit fixed asap. I figured she was hustling up the money for a revision, because Lord knows she needed it.

This cock-blocking ass bitch better beat it 'fore I embarrass her ass.

From a distance, I watched as she whispered something in his ear to which he shook his head. I assumed she'd asked him for a dance and he had turned her down. He then tucked a Grant in her garter belt before slapping her ass and sending her on her way.

Once the pathway was clear, I walked over and got his attention. "Hey, Mr. Asante..."

When he looked and saw that it was me he seemed a bit caught off guard. "Diana...?" He looked me up and down, from the tips of my stilettos to the top of my hair.

I was wearing my own shit in a cute, shoulder length blunt cut. I didn't fuck with them weaves and sew-ins anymore.

"Didn't expect seeing you here," he said.

"Likewise," I replied.

"Damn, Soul...Who is *this*?" Quest asked, sipping from a double Styrofoam cup.

Soul answered him in a dialect that I didn't understand. Before today, I didn't even know he spoke a second language. While they were talking, I peeped the Versace chain, belt, and Versace boots he was wearing. Whatever he said made Quest smile and nod his head at me. I figured he must've told him that he knew me from prison.

Suddenly, Dynasty walked over to make sure that no other hoes were pushing up on her man. Quest only showed love to her, and she'd be damned if another bitch got so much as a dollar off of him.

"Hey, baby," she said, kissing his cheek. "Wassup, boo. Lemme squeeze through."

I stepped to the side so she could come in the already crowded section.

"*Unh-unh!* Some of ya'll hoes gotta go!" she said to the other girls.

Dynasty was my girl and the only dancer I really fucked with in Persuasion's. She was a tall, pretty light skinned girl with a slender frame and gigantic ass. I always told her she looked like a damn Avatar with ass shots but the niggas loved her.

After Quest and Dynasty walked off together, I asked him, "Who is he to you?" He and Quest favored each other but Quest was darker in complexion. They had the same green eyes.

"You need not concern yourself with who he is," Mr. Asante said.

I looked at him and smiled. "You right...Besides...I may be interested in someone else..."

Mr. Asante licked his lips and grinned a little. The black tee he wore hugged his upper body, showing off his bulging chest and arms. I wanted to climb his ass like a tree, he was so damn fine. And I loved how he was low key with his shit. Not throwing money and acting all crazy like the other niggas in his section. He was chilling, just sipping on his glass of Hennessey without a care in the world.

"You been staying outta trouble?" he asked me.

I lied and said, "Yes."

He chuckled, showing off his dimples. "You so full of shit."

"You gon' buy me some diapers?" I teased.

His eyes twinkled with amusement. Clearly, he was entertained...and he hadn't even seen me up on stage yet.

"So... *Soul*? That's what they call you, huh? Or should I still address you as *sir*?"

He chuckled, appreciative of my memory. "Since I'm out of my work uniform, you can call me Soul."

"Speaking of which...it's nice to see what you look like out of it."

He winked at me. "Right back at'chu."

I started blushing like a little girl. It had been a while since a man had that effect on me. "So...are you ever gonna tell me how you got those marks?" I asked in reference to the scars on his face.

Soul paused for a minute, debating on whether or not he wanted to say. "They're tribal markings," he finally said. "They were given to me at a young age, so I've had them most of my life."

"You wouldn't tell me the first time I asked. That means we're making progress."

"...And what are we progressing towards?"

I shrugged my shoulders innocently. "I don't know. Maybe friends...maybe more..."

Suddenly, the DJ called my name to let me know that I needed to be on standby. I was up next after the twins, Yoshi and Yara. They were cleaning house while dancing to Future's "*Real Sisters*".

"Well...it was good seeing you," I said. "Don't be a stranger..."

"Don't worry," he said. "You'll be seeing me around."

23
SOUL

I couldn't keep my eyes off of Diana as I watched her switch to the stage. She had a stride that commanded attention from every nigga in the room. *Damn.* Baby girl was holding.

I shouldn't have been looking as hard as I was, considering that she was a former inmate, but it was difficult not to. Diana was thick all over and naturally pretty without even trying.

She had soft mocha brown skin, naturally long lashes, and a baby face that was the opposite of her demeanor. There was an edge to her; a cleverness about her that I appreciated. She was feisty, witty and funny. The fact that she was also beautiful was just an added bonus.

Drake and Future's *"Plastic Bag"* started playing as she grabbed the pole and seductively twirled around it. As much as I wanted to enjoy the show, I had too much respect for her as a person and as a woman to do so.

I guess that's my cue to bounce.

After dapping up the fellas and hugging my brother Quest, I excused myself from the crowded section. He tried to convince me to stay and get a dance but I lied and told him that I had an early shift the next day.

Quest lived in the mothafucking strip clubs. It was his home away from home. And though I would've loved to stay and indulge, I had a certain *obligation* waiting for me back at the crib.

Before walking out, I turned around and stole a quick glance at the stage. Diana was upside down with her legs suspended in the air, a flurry of bills pouring down on her like a rainstorm.

Get a plastic bag...

Go ahead and pick up all the cash...

Go ahead and pick up all the cash...

You danced all night, girl you deserve it...

She was good at being bad and bad at being good.

Our eyes met for a brief second...and in that moment, I felt like we were the only two people in the room. Like every nigga fanning ones in her face wasn't there and she only saw me. But the moment ended abruptly when Diana looked away. She then went back to performing for her many paying customers as if that were her only aspirations in life.

I wanted to see her have more.

But she would have to want more for herself.

24
RICO

On my way inside Persuasion's, I almost bumped into the nigga Soul. I knew him through a mutual friend but we didn't fuck with each other. That much was evident when he mean-mugged the fuck out of me on his way out.

Instead of reacting, I simply shook my head and laughed him off. I didn't pop duds and I didn't fight niggas. I counted money. And as long as someone didn't fuck up my count, we were cool.

He don't want no smoke, I thought to myself.

Like always, I kept that heat on me just in case a nigga felt foolhardy.

That night, I was rolling solo since I opted to leave my bitches in Miami. I knew that Diana wasn't ready to see them. Shit, she probably wasn't ready to see me either but I'd given her ass more than enough space.

Now it was time for her to come home...where she belonged.

To my amazement, I found her on stage popping her pussy for a bunch of niggas that couldn't afford her even if they cleaned out their savings.

She ain't playin' me. She playin' herself.

Standing off in the cut, I patiently waited for her turn on stage to end. A pair of strippers passed me by and smiled, obviously looking to make a come up off a nigga that was draped in all designer. The $300,000 watch on my wrist had their pussies dripping wet. They thought I had a couple hundreds for them, but sadly they were mistaken.

"Wassup baby? You wanna dance?" the shorter one asked.

I looked at them both in disgust. "I wouldn't spit on ya'll ugly ass hoes. Get the fuck out my face."

Insulted, they walked off with attitudes but not before cursing me out.

Oh well.

It's better to be hated for what you are, than to be loved for something you aren't.

I couldn't make boss moves without boss bitches.

Niggas always asked me why I never got involved in the drug game. I told them it was because the math never made sense to me. I'd ball for three years and then get sentenced to prison for twenty.

That's why I stayed in my lane.

When Diana saw me standing off to the side, she rolled her eyes at me. She didn't think she'd see me again after that shit she pulled at the diner. I was finally here to collect my payment—and that was her.

After Diana's turn ended, she climbed down with the assistance of one of her groupies. I hung back for a second because I wasn't about to compete for her attention. That wasn't something a man of my caliber was known for doing.

When Diana passed by she rolled her eyes at me a second time, clearly annoyed by my presence. She tried to go into the dressing room to freshen up but I grabbed her by the elbow to stop her.

"Aye. Hold up."

"What, Rico?"

"You ain't got nothing to say for that shit you pulled?"

She pretended to have amnesia. "What shit did I pull?"

"Don't play stupid. You ran off with my mothafucking car."

"You call it running off. I call it reparations. I think it's safe to say we're even now."

I turned her loose so that the security guard standing nearby didn't get the wrong impression. "You always was a petty bitch. I get you out and that's how you do me?"

"You did it to yourself," she said,

preparing to walk off.

Grabbing her arm again, I whirled her around to face me. "How long we gon' play this game for, Diana? All this childish shit ain't doing nothing but working us both the fuck up. Come home," I told her. "It's time to get back to making real money."

"No thank you, Rico. I'm managing just fine on my own."

"You just said the key word '*managing*.' What you need to be doing is '*maintaining*'," I told her. "You can work hard. But if you don't work smarter, you'll work hard for the rest of ya life."

"You know what, Rico? I'mma tell you something...You make it sound real good at rehearsal."

"Well...you know what they say. Practice makes perfect."

"Nigga, you so full of shit."

I chuckled in amusement. "See. That's yo' mothafucking problem. You too caught up on yo' mothafucking emotions. That's why I don't live off emotions. 'Cuz fucking around with yo' emotions, you'll be on all type of shit. And if you can't control your emotions, you can't control your money."

"I'm not too caught up on my emotions," she said. "I'm too caught up on the fact that you already betrayed me once—"

"Man, ain't nobody put a fucking gun to your head! No one forced you to make money with me! You were loving every single minute of that shit. You knew what'chu was getting yaself into. You knew the risk—"

"Yeah...I did...And it's a risk I never wanna take again."

There was a long period of silence between us.

"Who else gon' do you better than me?" I asked her. "Who else gon' put you in a position to make millions? Who gon' put you in foreign cars? Have you living out of mansions? Traveling the country...taking you on shopping sprees, spending thousands."

Diana laughed. "See? That's *your* problem," she said. "You too damn materialistic and superficial."

"Then go get'chu a broke nigga."

She smiled mischievously. "How you know I *ain't* checking for another nigga?"

I ain't like the sound of that at all, and it took everything in me not to slap the shit out of that hoe. She knew how a mothafucka felt about sharing. "A nigga don't value they life if they fucking around with you."

25
ROXIE

"Wow! I love this one!" Hae-Won said with excitement. The price tag on the wedding dress in her hands was a staggering $400,000. "What do you think about this?"

I didn't answer right away because my mind was in another place. I wasn't thinking about a marriage. I was thinking about how I was going to get the fuck out of Seoul.

"What do you think about it?" Hae-Won repeated.

I forced a smile. "It's lovely..."

"I wasn't talking to you, *amkae!*" she hissed.

Did she just call me a bitch? I didn't speak Korean fluently but I knew enough to know that.

"I was speaking to my *sister.*" She emphasized the last word to stress that I would never be apart of her family. Little did she know, I didn't want the responsibility.

"It's nice...But she'll definitely have to lose a couple pounds before the wedding if she plans on fitting in it," Dae said with an evil grin. She was the youngest sibling at only 18 and just as wicked as her sisters. Kwon had five of them in total but Seung was never around. I had never even seen any pictures of her, and as far as I knew she was an urban myth. Considering how cruel the other sisters were, maybe it was for the better that we didn't.

Hae-Won, Sun, and Gi all laughed at my misery.

"I can lose weight. But there's no hope for you and your fucked up ass family."

My comment shut every single one of their asses up.

WHAP!

Hae-Won smacked the shit out of me. I never saw it coming.

Blood leaked from my nose and dripped onto my t-shirt. I couldn't believe she'd actually hit me. It was her first time ever putting her hands on me. And though I wanted to fuck her up, I knew that Kwon would kill me if I did.

He made them keep an eye on me whenever he was out handling business, and each time they made my life a living hell. It was like they got a kick out of being mean or saying hurtful things to me. They knew I wouldn't do anything about it because I didn't want Kwon to hurt me or Rain.

Fear had broken me and now I was afraid to even defend myself. To make matters worse, I was being forced to marry a man that I no longer loved. Things couldn't have been any more fucked up.

Every day that I woke up in bed with him, I asked myself how I allowed this to happen? I felt like I was trapped in a prison. Not only was my life in danger but the life of my daughter's was as well.

All four sisters started speaking in Korean and I assumed they were saying all types of ignorant, racist shit about me. They didn't even try to hide their dislike for me. They loved picking me apart.

His sisters were so envious of me you would've thought they were fucking him. I didn't understand the hate and to be quite frank, I wasn't trying to. I had to find a way to get out of Korea—and soon, because there was no way in hell I was going to be the wife of a misfit.

***

When I got back home, I couldn't wait to spend time with my daughter. Rain was the only good thing about my life; the only positive influence on me. It was because of her that I chose to stay strong.

Rain was fast asleep in an expensive black walnut crib that Kwon had imported. Even though I didn't agree with his lifestyle or decision to force me into marriage, I couldn't deny that he treated my daughter exceptionally, and for that I was thankful. I'd gladly take the abuse—be it verbal or physical—as long as it meant that my child was safe. I'd die before I allowed one of those bitches to harm her.

Standing over Rain's crib, I watched as she slept peaceful and soundlessly. She was so beautiful. The apple of my eye.

I started humming a tune that my mother used to sing to me as a child. Rubbing her cheek as she hibernated, I admired how perfect she was. With her warm French vanilla skin, deep blue eyes, and piercing dimples, she was as cute as a cabbage patch doll.

Damn.

I can't let her grow up around all this fucked up shit—

My humming was suddenly interrupted by the sound of movement behind me. When I turned around, Kwon was standing in the doorway, leaning up against the frame. "Don't stop on my account," he said.

I hesitated to continue. Just him being around made me nervous. I cherished the moments when he wasn't home even though I was left with his crazy ass sisters. When he realized that I wouldn't continue, he walked over towards me.

"The girls tell me you've found a dress."

I grimaced at the misunderstanding. "*They* found it," I corrected him.

"Either way, it's great news," he said.

"How so?" I shot back.

"Well, now that you have the dress, we

can push the date for the wedding up. Don't you wanna tie the knot sooner?" he asked.

I looked at his ass like he was crazy. That was a trait that obviously seemed to run in his family. "Do you want the truth...or do you want me to lie?"

Kwon narrowed his eyes. "Whichever makes me happier...I suppose."

The close proximity made the hairs on back of my neck stand. He was intimidating without even trying. Threatening without having to utter a single threat. Kwon had me fearing for my life and I wanted nothing more than for him to leave me alone.

"Yes...I do..." I lied, not wanting to be next on the chopping block.

Pleased with my response, he leaned in and kissed me on the forehead. "Good...Now get cleaned up. Dinner's ready..."

***

"Can we talk about your sisters?"

Kwon and I were seated alone at the oak dining table with a plethora of food dishes in front of us. Chefs had prepared Korean fried chicken, Kalguksu, skewers, and egg bread. To wash it all down was a $10,000 bottle of Ace of Spades.

Unlike before, I wasn't impressed by his lavish lifestyle. It meant nothing to me if I didn't have my freedom. Kwon threw away my phone, had me chaperoned on the regular, and forbade me from speaking to anyone he didn't approve of first.

I may as well be his mothafucking house slave, I thought.

"What about them would you like to discuss?"

"Do you really think it's necessary for them to...babysit me? Last time I checked I was a grown ass woman."

Kwon smiled and wagged a finger at me. "Last time I left you alone you tried to run," he reminded me. "Now we can't have that again...especially before the wedding."

I choked back tears hearing him say that. "Kwon...I can't live like this," I cried. "I'm miserable. I'm mistreated. I'm lonely and I'm afraid!"

"Fine. I'll get you a dog."

"I don't want a dog! I wanna go home!"

"STOP THIS!" Kwon slammed his fists on the table so hard that the silverware rattled. "This is your home! We're getting married! And that's the end of it! I don't wanna hear this shit everyday! Do I make myself clear?"

I nodded my head sheepishly.

"I can't hear you."

"...Yes..."

"Right now I need you out of my presence," he said, dismissively. "Now leave..."

"But...I haven't eaten anything—"

"A meal is a privilege. And quite frankly you haven't earned it."

My stomach started rumbling like crazy. "Are you serious?"

Kwon's jaw tightened in anger and his right hand slowly moved towards the knife on the table. Two of his fingers twitched, presumably itching to grab it and stab the life out of me. Suddenly, images of Jag stabbing me flashed across my mind.

"Do you really wanna test me?" Kwon asked.

This was the first time I had ever truly seen his bad side.

Gulping in fear, I shook my head no.

"Then don't make me repeat myself," he said in a stern tone.

Standing to my feet, I prepared to excuse myself.

"Roxie?" he called out just seconds before I left the room.

I stopped in my tracks and turned around to face him.

"Aren't you forgetting something."

I looked at him in confusion."

"My goodnight kiss," he said.

Now he was just fucking with me for the hell of it. Taking my time, I walked over to him and leaned down to give him a peck. From the corner of my eye, I noticed the knife sitting in front of him. I thought about reaching for it until Kwon said something that changed my mind.

"You're free to make whatever choice you want, but you are not free from the consequences of that choice."

26
MAGYC

That day, I decided to spend the afternoon with my son Marlon. Tara was always on my ass about how I never came to see him, so I picked him up in the morning and had been with him since. After breakfast at I-Hop, I took him to the aquarium to see the dolphin show and then to the zoo. We were walking through the gorilla exhibit when Cameron called me out of the blue.

Automatically, I found it odd because she rarely if ever reached out to me. Normally, I only dealt with her husband Jude so I couldn't figure out why she was hitting me up all of a sudden.

"Wus good, boss lady?"

"I've been calling Roxie like crazy and this chick ain't been answering none of my calls or texts. Then when I hit her up a few days ago, I saw that her phone was disconnected. She ain't posted to Instagram in over a month...and all this shit is just odd. I don't think it's a coincidence. This ain't like her at all. What's going on?"

"Yeah...well, she ran out the country with that nigga, in spite of what I told her. So if it's anybody you should be questioning, it's that slanted eyed mothafucka. I ain't checking for her moves no more. Me and her ain't got shit to do with each other." And I meant every word of it. My days of chasing a bitch who'd rather chase another nigga were over. If she wanted that mothafucka so bad she could have him. It was time for me to move on. I had other things to worry about besides Roxie. Like building my business from the ground up after the fucked up shit Kwon did.

"Magyc...this is serious. Whatever ya'll going through gon' have to wait. Put your emotions to the side and see what's up with her...because I just *know* something ain't right. I can just feel it in my heart," Cameron said. "We talk every other day, there's no way she'd change her number without giving it to me. It ain't like Roxie to go missing."

"Did she tell you she was leaving town with that nigga?" I asked her.

Cameron paused. "No..."

"That ain't like her either...Don't you agree?"

Cameron thought about it. "You're right..."

"Maybe you don't know Roxie as well as you think."

I damn sure didn't.

There was a brief period of silence.

"Or maybe there's something wrong. You *need* to look into it, Magyc. Because if she's in any trouble, and we neglected to look into it, I'd never forgive myself," she said. "Could you...?"

27

SOUL

Drake's "*Pop Style*" thumped through the speakers of Persuasion's Gentlemen's Club on a Thursday night. As soon as I walked in, I started scanning the crowd for her. On this particular evening, I wasn't there to politic with my brother. I'd come specifically looking for her...because as much as I hated to admit it, she had gotten under my skin.

Dropped outta school now we dumb rich...

This sound like some forty-three-oh-one shit...

All my niggas wanna do is pop style...

Turn my birthday into a lifestyle...

The spot was lit for a weekday. Heavy clouds of marijuana and hookah permeated the air, making the whole place foggy. *Damn. This bitch smoked out.*

They still out to get me, they don't get it...

I can not be got, and that's a given...

As *Pop Style* poured through the subwoofers, I searched the plethora of strippers for Diana. I wasn't supposed to be checking for her like this because of prison regulations. But I couldn't deny a nigga was curious about her.

I finally spotted Diana over by the bar,

talking to some older cat. When she saw me across the club, she smiled at me and winked.

I made myself comfortable at an empty table near the stage and ordered a straight shot of Hennessey. Firing up a cigarette, I waited for her to finish up. A couple strippers tried to holla but lap dances wasn't how I got down. Instead, I tipped them a few dollars and sent them on their way. Shortly after, Diana joined me with a glass of vodka and lime. She was peanut butter thick and looked enticing in a blue two piece.

It should've been a mothafucking sin to be that sexy.

Damn.

Look at me.

I shouldn't even fucking be here.

...And with her, of all people.

If my boss found out I was fucking a former inmate, I'd lose my job and credibility. But something about her made me want to risk it all. I was intrigued by her personality, drawn to her good looks. I didn't know a whole lot about her...but I knew there was more than meets the eye...and I wanted to know her story.

"I didn't think we'd run into each other again," she said.

"Why's that?"

"I don't know...Maybe 'cuz it's been two weeks since I've last seen you..."

The corner of my mouth curved into a grin. She made it sound like she missed a nigga. "I'mma busy man," I told her. "Between working at the prison and coaching football on the weekends, I don't get much downtime. And whenever I do, it's usually spent with my little lady."

Diana looked surprised. "*Little lady?*" she repeated. "So there's a woman in your life?" In her tone was a hint of disappointment.

"I wouldn't call her a woman...She's only eight."

"Wow. I didn't know you had a daughter. What's her name?"

"Her name's Madison."

"You got any pictures of Madison?"

"...Yeah." Reaching in my pocket, I pulled out my iPhone and unlocked it. I then went to my photo album, where there was nothing but pictures of Madison. All day she liked to play in my phone, taking hundreds of selfies.

I handed Diana the phone so she could see them.

"Oh my God, Soul! She's beautiful—and she's got your eyes."

"I hear that all the time."

"Do you got her spoiled? Be honest," she laughed.

"Yeah...She is pretty damn spoiled rotten. I wouldn't be surprised if right now she was giving the sitter hell."

Diana handed me the phone back. "Where's her mom?" she asked curiously.

I paused, debating on whether or not I wanted to say. It wasn't something I liked to talk about. "After Maddie was born she left."

"Oh...wow...So you've raised her since she was baby?"

"Absolutely."

"That's really commendable."

When I looked over her shoulder, I noticed a nigga staring hard as fuck in our direction. It was the same one from the bar and he looked like he wanted her attention back. "I think someone's waiting on you."

Diana turned around and looked at him. "A few more minutes won't hurt him," she said.

Suddenly, I felt like I was wasting her time with small talk. Peeling off a Franklin, I tried to give it to her but she stopped me.

"You don't have to pay me to see me," she said.

"Well, I don't wanna hold you up either. I just came to see how were you doing." I stood to my feet to leave. I then held my hand out for her to take. When she did, I tugged her up.

"So that's it?" she asked.

"What'chu mean that's it?"

"I only get to see you when I'm on the clock?"

"Where else am I supposed to see you, Diana?" I almost called her by her last name out of habit. I had to get used to the fact that she was no longer an inmate.

"I don't know...You tell me..." There was a twinkle in her eyes and flirtation in her smile.

"Shit, what'chu got movin' for the rest of the week?"

"I'm just taking it one move at a time."

"Cool. Let's exchange numbers. Maybe we can make some moves together."

28
ROXIE

"I'm flying to Atlanta to handle some business. I may be there a few days...depending on how smoothly everything runs."

I was sitting out back in the garden when Kwon came and delivered unexpected news.

"Why are you going there?" I asked him.

Kwon looked down at Rain in my arms. I was trying to teach her how to walk. "Are you sure you wanna know?"

I thought about how chilling it was to discover that he killed people and sold their organs. Maybe it was best that I didn't. Then I thought about it. Atlanta was greatly known for having a high percentage of kidnappings, particularly children.

"On second thought, I'd rather not," I told him.

Kwon continued to fix the collar of his dress shirt. As his soon-to-be-wife, it was my job to do things like that for him. But with the way I felt about him now, I wouldn't piss on his ass if he was on fire.

"On an unrelated note, I've hired coordinators to begin making preparations for our big day. It will be sometime next month."

"Why the rush?"

"Why delay?"

There was a lot I wanted to say but I held my tongue out of fear.

"Afterwards, we can immediately begin to work on conception."

"A *baby*?!" I practically spat the word out. He really must've lost his fucking mind if he thought I was going to give him a child. "I already have a baby, Kwon...Plus, it takes a lot of responsibility to raise a child. And you *clearly* have a lot going on."

"This isn't up for debate," he said. "Besides, I have something I wanna show you. Come to the family room with me. I've gotta surprise."

Kwon held his hand out for me to take and reluctantly I did.

Following him to the family room with Rain on my hip, I was curious to know what type of surprise he had in store for me.

In the middle of the room was an adorable little bundle sent from dog heaven. A white teacup maltipoo was nestled comfortably in its pet lounge.

I can't believe this mothafucka really got me a dog.

"He's cute," I said. "But he doesn't make my stay any less uncomfortable."

"Well, what can I do to change that?"

"How about you start trusting me to be alone?"

"Give me some time to consider that. When I get back, I'll give you an answer."

I had a feeling it'd be no regardless but it didn't hurt to ask.

After kissing me and Rain farewell, he left the house to head to the Incheon International Airport. As soon as I heard the front door close behind him, I left the room and tiptoed downstairs to see what his younger sister Dae was up to.

She'd fallen asleep on the sofa while watching a K-drama. Lying on the coffee table right in front of her was her iPhone 6s.

29
ROXIE

Removing my shoes, I tiptoed down the stairs and towards the mobile device. Dae was curled up on the sofa with her eyes closed and lips slightly parted. If it wasn't for the steady rising of her chest, I would've thought she was dead.

Making sure to be extra careful and quiet, I crept to the table and reached for the phone. Dae moved a little and my heartbeat went into overdrive. I just knew she was going to open her eyes and see me trying to steal her phone. But to my surprise, she didn't wake.

My fingers were less than two inches away when I heard the front door unlock. Assuming that it was Kwon, I bolted towards the staircase and out of view.

Shit! So much for me calling for help.

I figured that Kwon had left something behind. However, it wasn't him who walked in. Even worse, it was his sisters Hae-Won and Sun. With Kwon's sisters and the two armed security guards always stationed out front, I didn't know how I'd ever get out. And it was damn near impossible for anyone to get in.

Shit, I cursed.

When I finally reached the top of the

stairs, I almost bumped into Kwon's maid. A tiny glimmer of hope washed over me when I realized that she might be able to lend me her phone.

Grabbing her by the arm, I pulled her off to the side so that his sisters didn't see me talking to her. "I need to use the phone," I whispered. "Now—before they see me!"

"*Naneun yeong-eo leul moshaneun!*" she said alarmed.

"*Sssh!*" I quickly placed my index finger to my lips. If they caught us, we'd both be in trouble.

"All I want is to use your phone—or any phone! If you know where one is, or if you could get me one, I'd really appreciate it! Please!" I begged. I was finally desperate enough to ask for her help. She was my last resort.

"I—I don't speak any English," she said, shaking her head.

I wasn't buying her bullshit. "Your English sounds pretty damn good to me."

"Please, I—I don't want any trouble."

"And you won't get any. All I want is to use a phone. Please. I have to get out of here!"

"I can't—"

I quickly cut her off. "Do you have any kids?"

She nodded her head nervously. "A son..."

"And you'd do anything to protect your son, right?"

"Yes...Of course."

I gently placed my hand on her arm. "Please...I just wanna protect my baby. You and I both know this isn't a place for a child. I just want to get her far away from this crazy shit. But in order to do that, I need a phone to call for help."

She stared at me with sympathetic eyes. I could tell that she felt sorry for me. I saw it on her face each and every day...but like me, she was too afraid to speak up.

All of a sudden, she reached for her sleeves and slowly rolled them up. On her inner arms were gruesome keloid scars from where she'd been cut multiple times.

"Wha—who did this to you?" I asked in shock. "Did *he* do this to you?"

Tears filled her eyes. "They all did this to me..."

"*They?*"

"My brother...and my sisters..."

Suddenly, it dawned on me. "You're Seung?"

Tears rolled down her cheeks as she nodded.

"Why did they do this to you?"

"Because I didn't agree with what they were doing…" she said. "*Now* do you understand why I don't wanna get involved?"

It was my turn to look at her sympathetically.

Kwon was a monster. How could he do something so barbaric to his sister? If he was capable of doing this to his own flesh and blood, then there was no telling what all he'd do to me. I had to get me and my baby the fuck away from him.

"Help me…And I promise to get you out of here too."

"I have nowhere else to go," she admitted. "But I may be able to help you. Follow me."

Seung led me down the narrow hall to a door that was always locked. Pulling out her key ring, she found the proper one and unlocked the door. To my amazement, it was Kwon's office, equipped with a large bookcase, desk, and chaise lounge. On the desk was an Apple iMac desktop.

Seung quickly ran over to the laptop and powered it on. "He doesn't know that I know his access code. Occasionally, I sneak and use it to check on my son. It's the only way I can speak to him."

"Kwon forbids you from seeing your own son?"

"Kwon rules everything. No one can make

any moves before going through him first."

"You know, that's real sick. That's real fucked up."

"You must not know how fucked up my brother is."

Seung turned the computer screen towards me and I saw that my prayers had been answered. Kwon had a Skype account, which was abundantly convenient.

I immediately thought about calling the cops. "What's the emergency telephone number?" I asked her.

"It's no point in calling the police," she said. "Kwon has ties to most of the police departments and certain politicians as well. If you go to them for help, the only thing they'll do is turn you back over to him. You're better off calling someone else."

Without further delay, I punched in Magyc's cell phone number and waited for him to pick up.

30
MAGYC

I had just left out of the hospital after visiting my bro when my line rang. Looking at the caller ID, I noticed that it was some weird number. Assuming it was a telemarketer or some shit, I pressed the ignore button. I wasn't in the mothafucking mood for spammy calls. I had a lot on my mind, like my brother's health and the flight that I had to catch soon.

I was halfway to my car when it rang again. I started to hit ignore but something told me to answer so I did. "Who the fuck is this?"

"Magyc! Magyc, it's me!"

"Roxie?"

"I don't have much time to talk—so I need you to listen! They're downstairs and they don't know I'm using the phone."

"Who's they? And where the fuck you at? I been blowing you the fuck up!"

"I'm in Seoul. Kwon forced me to be here against my will! Rain and I are in danger! I need you to come and get us! I know I didn't listen but—"

Her voice trailed off.

"Rox?"

"Hold on. I think I hear somebody

coming," she whispered. After several seconds of silence, she continued, "False alarm. I thought it was one of them. Listen, I need you to come and get me. These people are very dangerous."

"Roxie, you mean to tell me you in Seoul with that crazy ass fool! I told you to stay away from that crazy ass mothafucka! And you allowed Rain to get caught up too. I can't believe you, Roxie. I'm disappointed in you."

"I know," she cried. "I know you tried to warn me! I know you did and I'm sorry I didn't listen. If I had, I wouldn't be here! But you don't know how good it is to hear your voice. Can you please come and get us, Magyc? Please, please, please. I don't have anyone else to rely on."

"Fuck it. None of that matters now. Where are you? Has he touched you? Has he hurt Rain? I swear if he laid a finger on you, I—"

"No. We're fine. It hasn't gotten that bad..." she paused. "Yet..."

"Look, I'm on my way to the airport right now! I need you to tell me exactly where you are! Don't leave out a single detail!"

Scribbling her address on an old receipt, I sent a text to my killers while she was still on the line, letting them know to meet me at the airport. I needed every one of them niggas for what I had in store for Kwon.

That's how he wanna play this shit? Aight then, I got something for that bitch.

"Okay, Roxie. I need you to listen to me very carefully. Don't give any indications that we ever spoke. We don't wanna raise any red flags. 'Cuz when I blow down on their asses, I don't want 'em to see it coming."

I was putting a bullet in that bitch and every single last mothafucka that was associated.

31
ROXIE

The following afternoon, I found myself in the study room, admiring the sword over the fireplace when Hae-Won walked in.

"You planning on using that?" she asked with a sly grin.

"I was just admiring how shiny and sharp the blade is."

Hae-Won leaned up against the wall and folded her arms. "It's something, isn't it? Once belonged to my father," she explained. "He was a great man, god rest his soul."

"May I ask what happened to him?"

"He died...of pancreatic cancer."

I was shocked to hear that because Kwon had never mentioned it. As a matter of fact, he'd led me to believe his father was still alive. Then again, he'd also led me to believe that he was sane.

"I know what you're thinking," she said. "But we couldn't save him. By the time doctors made the discovery, it had already spread."

"...I'm sorry to hear that."

Hae-Won looked at me and frowned. "Please don't patronize me with your fake ass sympathy. It's insulting."

"You're right," I agreed. "I'm not sorry. And I'm also not sorry about what's gonna happen to you and your sisters."

Hae-Won looked amused. "What's gonna happen to me and my sisters?" she asked. "Do tell."

"I won't have to. You'll see soon enough."

Hae-Won smiled and unfolded her arms. "You know what? When I first met you, I couldn't help but wonder what my brother saw in you. You seemed weak, naïve, and quite frankly not that attractive," she said. "But now I see why he's so taken by you. I'll admit it...You've got heart..."

I proudly stood my ground as she took several steps towards me.

"But if you threaten me again, you won't have that heart. I'll cut it out of you myself and feed it to your daughter—"

"Bitch, don't fucking speak on my child!"

She opened her mouth to say something but was interrupted by the sudden sound of gunshots outside.

POP!

POP!

BOOM!

BOOM!

32

ROXIE

After several gunshots went off a loud bang rang out, followed by more gunfire. Realizing that they were now in the house, Hae-Won took off running towards the source of the noise. But not before grabbing a loaded gun out of the top drawer of the media console.

Once she left, I bolted towards the next room, which was Rain's. She was crying and screaming at the top of her lungs. Grabbing her out of the crib, I covered her ears with my hands.

I heard the sound of scuffling along with porcelain statues and vases breaking. The battle downstairs must've been an intense one and I prayed that Magyc was okay. I should've told him to exercise caution upon arrival. All of Kwon's sisters knew martial arts and they were all handy when it came to using a blade. As a tradition in his family, it was mandatory.

Even with me trying my best to shield her from the noise, Rain hollered, cried, and flung her arms wildly. She was having an uncontrollable fit. Suddenly, Seung ran inside the room and slammed the door shut. "Here," she said, handing me a tiny handgun. "Take it...just in case you need it."

I accepted the gun even though I didn't want to have to use it.

POP!

POP!

POP!

BOOM!

Gunfire continued to go off downstairs and I could only hope that it was Magyc's. If the sister's succeeded, then Kwon would cut me and my baby up.

"I'll be back," Seung said, preparing to leave.

I quickly grabbed her wrist to stop her. "No!"

"I promise I'll come right back to check on you."

Despite my pleas, she left the room—taking two to the chest as soon as she walked out.

"*Noooooo!*" I cried out.

Trying to avoid being hit by the gunfire, I ran towards Seung and pulled her back into the bedroom. Blood quickly soaked her shirt; the wounds were fatal. "Hold on!" I said anyway. "Just hold on! I'm gonna get you some help!" Grabbing Rain's blanket out of the crib, I applied pressure to her wounds—but it was no use. She was already gone.

After several more seconds, the gunshots finally came to a halt. Because I didn't know the outcome of the war, I sat in the corner of the room, protecting my child with the gun in my hand.

All of a sudden, the door to the room opened, and my first instinct was to point my gun at whoever was walking in. I breathed a shaky sigh of relief when I saw that it was Magyc.

He had a semi-automatic in his hand and his shirt was covered in blood. One of them had cut him pretty badly but it didn't look life threatening. "Magyc!" I was beyond grateful to see him. He was a godsend.

Running up to him, I flung my arm around his neck while holding Rain with the other. He held both of us tight. I could smell the sweat and gunpowder on his skin.

"Come on. Let's get the fuck up outta here!" Magyc said, pulling me towards the door.

"Okay." I was somewhat frantic.

We were just about to walk out when he stopped suddenly. "Hold up..." Magyc looked down at Seung's dead body. "You and Rain don't need to see what's out there," he said.

I figured it must've been bad for him to say that. Nodding my head in agreement, I covered Rain's eyes and closed my own. Magyc gently took me by the arm and carefully led me out of the room. The house was quiet, eerily quiet. I didn't even hear the sound of the dog barking, which led me to believe they had killed it.

Suddenly, I bumped into what I assumed was someone's arm or leg. Magyc kicked whoever and whatever it was out of the way. "Don't worry. I got'chu," he said.

When I heard the sound of nearby movement, I almost freaked out but he told me that it was his boys. It sounded like they were ransacking the place, looking for whatever valuables they could find. I'd forgotten that he hung with nothing but street niggas.

On the way to the front door, I slipped on something wet and almost fell—but Magyc quickly grabbed me and Rain before I lost my balance.

"Almost there," he said.

When I felt the concrete under my soles, I knew that we were finally outside. "Is it safe to open my eyes now?" I asked.

"Not yet," he said.

Magyc led me all the way to his car, where he opened the door and ushered us inside.

"I'mma need you to take 'em home for me," he told his driver.

That's when my eyes shot open. "Wait! What? You're not coming with us?!"

"There's something else I need to take care of."

"Kwon's not here!" I told him.

"Where the fuck is he then?"

"He flew to the states. To Atlanta."

"Well, that's where I'm headed—"

"Magyc, you don't have to do this. I don't want you chasing after his crazy ass. It's done already. Just let it go—"

"It's far from done. Do you know what I just did? I started an all out war! I need to get you and Rain somewhere safe 'cuz I don't want ya'll caught in the crossfire."

"Maybe I can help. I know where we might be able to find him."

33
SOUL

"Come on! Come on! Hustle, hustle, hustle!" I had all the boys doing scramble drills with leg resistance bands to work on increasing their speed. Since football had always been a passion of mine, I took up coaching for a high school out in Buford, Georgia. It was an hour drive to and back but what I got out of it was so worth it.

Having a rough upbringing, I knew how easy it was for a young, black male to fall prey to the street life. I didn't want that for my boys so I pushed them to train and play hard so they could one day make it big.

Because I'd sold drugs most of my life, I didn't have the same opportunities presented to me as they did—and I didn't want to see them go down the same path as me and Quest. So I did everything in my power to keep them focused and out of the trouble.

After leg drills, I had them practice blocking, tackling and linebacker drills. I worked their asses so hard that one of them threw up from exhaustion. Though it may've been tough love, one day they would thank me.

My daughter came over and brought them each an ice cold bottle of water. She was unashamedly a daddy's girl, who was just as passionate about the sport as I was. Madison was to me what Riley Curry was to her dad Stephen. She came to all of the practice sessions and games with me and even watched the playoffs when it came on TV.

I watched as a few of the boys exchanged hi-fives with her. They loved Maddie and treated her like she was their little sister. Since they were all preoccupied, I decided to step off to the side to make a phone call.

Diana's line rang several times and when she didn't answer, I assumed that she was busy. I started to leave her a short and simple voicemail but suddenly her sultry voice filled the receiver. "Hello?"

"Did I hit you at a bad time?"

"No...I just got out of the shower."

Images of her naked body dripping with beads of water flooded my mind. I had to clear my throat just to get my composure together. "What'chu getting into tonight?" I asked.

"I don't know yet. No plans."

"You ain't going to the spot?"

"Nah, probably not."

"How 'bout dinner tonight?"

I could hear her smiling through the phone. "That sounds like a plan."

"Tell me...what's one of your favorite

foods?"

Diana paused to think about it. "I love steak."

"Well then, steak it is."

34

DIANA

It was a quarter after 8 when I pulled up into a beautiful gated community in Alpharetta, Georgia. The address Soul had given me led me to a newly built Craftsman home on the corner of a quiet cul de sac. At least it looked like it was newly built, judging from the structure.

Parked in his driveway was a Ducati motorcycle and a black Audi RS5. From what I could tell, Soul looked like he was doing well for himself. Being a correctional officer and part-time football coach must've paid nicely.

After parking behind his Audi, I turned off the engine and climbed out of my car. Admiring the neatly trimmed lawn, I made my way towards the front of the house. Soul was already waiting for me at the door with the sexiest grin on his face, and I assumed it was because he liked what he saw.

I was wearing the hell out of a nude ribbed dress and gold sandals. My hair was flat ironed bone straight and hung just a little past my shoulders. My makeup and jewelry was minimal, and accentuating the entire fit was a gold-studded beige Louboutin clutch.

"I've gotta get used to seeing you in regular clothes," he said.

I handed him the bottle of wine I was carrying. "Right back at'cha."

Soul looked handsome that day in a short sleeve white button down, black slacks, and Nike trainers.

"Should I take my shoes off?" I asked him.

"Whatever makes you more comfortable."

Since I wore heels damn near every night, I pulled them off without a second thought. To my surprise, Soul's floors were heated. "Wow. This is a nice place you have," I said, admiring the layout, furniture, and artwork. Crown molding, ceiling lights, and dark hardwood floors were spread throughout. The Internet's *"Partners in Crime, Pt. 2"* was playing softly through the built-in Bluetooth speakers. Not only did the place look clean, it smelled clean too.

"Thank you," he said.

"Everything's so neat too. You must have OCD."

Soul chuckled. "Growing up, my folks stayed on me about cleanliness. And you know what they say. Train up a child in the way he should go, and when he is old he will not depart from it."

"Amen," I said. "Speaking of child, where's your daughter."

"With a friend."

"Aww, too bad. I would've loved to meet

her."

"Next time," he said.

I tossed him a flirtatious smile. "So there's a next time."

"Depends on how you act..."

I laughed him off. "Whatever. Anyway, where's this dinner you promised me?" I certainly didn't smell any steak.

Soul led me to the kitchen, where I expected a full course meal to be laid out. Instead, a package of raw steaks and assorted vegetables were on the counter, waiting to be prepared.

"What part of the game is this?" I asked. "I expected the food to be done."

Soul walked up behind me and placed an apron around my waist. "And I expect you to know your way around a kitchen."

"Are you serious?" I laughed.

"Dead ass."

I turned around and looked at him—and that's when I realized his eyes changed colors. Instead of mint green, they were now light brown with tiny specks of gray.

"I'll cook for you," I agreed. "But you gotta do something for me first."

"What do you want me to do?"

"...I wanna ask you a couple questions and I want you to answer 'em." I felt like I had to hit him with the ultimatum because he wasn't willingly giving up the info about himself. Soul was mysterious, and while that did initially attract me to him, I also wanted to know who I was dealing with.

"You can ask me anything," he said.

"Okay...well...for starters...how old are you?"

"Thirty."

"...Back at the club—when I saw you there for the first time, you were speaking another language. What language was that?"

"I'm Ghanaian, and I was speaking Twi. It's a widely spoken language in Ghana."

"Tree?" I repeated.

"Twi," he pronounced again.

"Wow. I had no idea you were African."

"Any other questions you got for me?"

"Yeah...How do you know Quest?"

"Aight, now you asking *too* many questions," he said. There was a hint of humor in his tone that let me know he wasn't too serious.

"You told me I could ask you anything."

Soul released a deep breath and ran a hand over his waves. He was becoming increasingly frustrated by my curiosity. "He's my brother," he finally said. "Anything else?"

"I need to know what type of shit ya'll into. I can look at Quest and tell he's trouble."

Soul laughed. "All these questions about Quest. I'm starting to think you'd rather be cooking dinner for him."

I sensed a little jealousy in his voice, and to be real, I found it kind of cute. Wrapping my arms around his neck, I looked him dead in the eyes. "I'm with who I want."

I leaned in to kiss him but he stopped me.

"If you want me, you gon' have to change your profession."

35
DIANA

For dinner, I made steak with stuffed portabella mushrooms, garlic roasted broccoli, and rosemary potatoes. I may've been a drop out and a stripper, but I could cook my ass off in the kitchen, thanks to my grandmother. I didn't even have to ask Soul if he enjoyed the food, because it was evident from how spotless his plate was left.

After dinner, we cleaned the dishes together and talked about our lives and goals. His dream was to put his daughter through college and see his boys play professional ball. Mine was to one day own a restaurant.

Once the kitchen was clean, I packaged up the leftovers and put them in the fridge. As soon as I closed it, Soul was standing right behind me. All of a sudden, and without warning, he backed me up against it.

Leaning down, he pressed his soft lips to mine. The kiss caught me off guard, and I accidentally let out a whimper in response. Soul wrapped his massive hands around my tiny waist as he pulled me towards him. We were so close that I could feel his erection pressing into me.

"Put your arms around my neck," he whispered.

I complied and yelped a little when he lifted me off my feet. Carrying me over to the kitchen island, he placed me on the counter top and slid between my legs. My mind said no but my eyes screamed fuck me. I wanted him more anything. Hell, I'd wanted him since the very first time that I saw him.

Soul gently wrapped his hand around my neck as the kiss deepened. I loved how he was a healthy combination of passionate and aggressive.

When I grabbed onto his thick, meaty dick, he started breathing hard. "You sure we ain't moving too fast?" he asked in a hoarse tone.

I smiled at his thoughtfulness while reaching for his belt. "I've been locked up for over year and I haven't had *any* since I got out. Feels like we aren't moving fast enough."

Soul grabbed my face and kissed me harder, biting and nibbling on my bottom lip. He was rough, but sweet. Rapacious, but tender. Pushing me back onto the counter, he spread my legs and slipped my panties off. Tugging him down with me by his shirt, we kissed again—like we couldn't get enough of each other. I needed him...and all ten of his inches deep inside me.

"Fuck me..." I pleaded.

After freeing his wood, Soul rested the tip just against my base. "As you wish..."

He was just about to stick it in when his

phone started ringing. "Ignore it," I told him.

Soul looked over at the caller ID. "I can't," he said. "It's my baby girl. I'm sorry but I gotta take this."

"No, it's...totally understandable," I said, struggling to not sound disappointed.

After quickly fixing his clothes, he answered the phone. "Wassup, Princess?" Soul put his daughter on speaker.

"Daddy, can you come and get me. *Pleeeease!* I'm *soooo* bored. There's nothing to do at old people's houses...except stare out the window and count the peppermints in the candy dish. I wanna come home," she whined.

Soul wasn't lying when he said she was spoiled.

"Don't let Miss Orr hear you calling her old," he said.

"Please, daddy, come and get me."

"Yeah, okay...I'll come and get'chu," he agreed.

Sliding off the counter, I slid back into my panties since it was clear that I wasn't gonna get any.

"Alright, love. See you soon," he said before hanging up.

I was just about to leave the room when he gently grabbed me by the wrist and pulled me towards him. "Where you think you going?" Grabbing me by the throat, he kissed me intensely. He was physically dominating, but damn did it turn me on.

"You'd better stop before you get something started. And ain't no sense in starting nothing you can't finish."

Soul chuckled. "What'chu doing this weekend?" he asked. "I wanna take you somewhere."

"Where you wanna take me?"

"You'll see this weekend...So don't make no other plans."

36

KWON

A$AP Rocky's "*Electric Body*" poured through the speakers inside of Persuasion's on a Friday. I was there because my boys had thrown me a bachelor's party, and there was no better city for fun and adult entertainment than Atlanta. Not only did I get a sizeable amount of my victims from the city, but women practically threw themselves at me.

They saw my flashy cars and designer clothes and they knew that I was rich. They had no idea that it was because I sold human organs.

As cruel and vicious as it was, sometimes I even kidnapped women that I courted to have them killed and later on disemboweled. To be honest, that was my initial plans for Roxie...but she was different.

Somewhere along the way, I got lost.

I fell in love, obsessive love. And it'd gotten so bad that it eventually overpowered what was once genuine. Instead of feeling the same about me, Roxie feared me. But it didn't matter. I was certain that one day she would learn to love me again. Now that I had her right where I wanted her, I wasn't letting her go. Ever.

"Hey, SeoKwon, 11:00," Jisoo said, interrupting my thoughts.

He was one of my closest friends, and the lead director of my "hijacking" team. Anytime I needed bodies, he and his men went out to get them and he was faithful with meeting his quota for every "supply run". Jisoo was also the one who introduced me to Roxie.

Turning my head in the direction he'd indicated, I noticed a beautiful woman with mocha skin and shoulder length hair. She had an array of tattoos all over her curvy body and a cute, little baby face.

She looked absolutely stunning.

"Bring her to me," I told him. Our section was already crammed with half-naked women but it wasn't a party without her.

Jisoo wasted no time as he went to fetch her the same way that I had him fetch Roxie. As I waited for him to bring her over, my second phone started vibrating. Usually, it only rang when it was something business-related—and tonight, business wasn't a main priority.

I was enjoying myself and I figured whatever it was could wait. Ignoring the call, I watched as Jisoo whispered something in the dancer's ear and pointed in my direction.

I'd killed so many unsuspecting women that way it was ridiculous. After luring them in with promises of a good time, I'd convince them to leave with me. Within forty-eight hours, they were lying on a cold, metal table with their chest cavities opened and their hearts, livers, and kidneys missing.

I had become so used to murdering people that I no longer felt any sympathy for taking an innocent life, be it man, woman, or child. I'd allowed this lifestyle and family business to turn me cold and sinister.

When I looked over in Jisoo's direction, I noticed him and the dancer making their way over towards me. "He's right here," he said, pointing at me. "He's never had a dance before so take it easy on him." That was one of his most famous lines.

"Hey, there," she waved. "I heard you're getting married soon. Congratulations!"

I bowed out of curtesy. "Thank you."

"Isn't this your bachelor party? You don't look like you're having too much fun," she noted.

I found it so amusing how rehearsed these stripper bitches were. Roxie had said something ironically similar back when we first met. It was like they'd all read the same book and practiced the same bullshit.

"That's 'cuz *you* weren't here," I said, matching her game.

She squinted her eyes a little as if she were scrutinizing me. "Yo, you look *sooo* familiar. I don't know why."

"Don't tell me you're one of those

stereotypes who thinks all Asians look the same," I joked.

She laughed. "Of course not. It's just— wait! Oh! I know where I know you from. You're Roxie's dude, right?"

"Technically, I'm her fiancé," I corrected.

"*Riiight.* I thought I recognized you," she said.

There was a long, awkward silence between us before she spoke again.

"Well...it was good seeing you. Again, congrats."

She started to walk off but I softly latched onto her wrist. "Wait a minute. Where're you running off to so soon? I didn't even get your name..."

"Diana...but everybody here calls me Juicy."

"I certainly see why."

My compliment made her bashful.

"I'm Kwon."

"I know who you are. And I also know it ain't right to be all up in your face like this. You're my girl's fiancé."

"Your *girl*? Funny...she never talks about you."

Diana cut her eyes at me. She didn't like to hear that.

"All I want is a dance..." I told her.

"There's plenty other girls you can choose from."

"None of them look like you though."

"Kwon—"

"It's just a dance," I repeated, easing her onto my lap. She was incredibly soft, almost like baby's skin. I lightly touched her chest to feel her heartbeat. "It's racing..."

"You got me nervous..."

"Don't be."

"Hard not to."

It gradually slowed down and became normal again. "You have a healthy heart," I smiled.

Diana looked confused. Before she could ask what I meant, her attention was stolen by a man who'd just walked in. "Oh my God," she said unenthused. "Excuse me for a moment."

Diana quickly climbed off of me and disappeared inside the dressing room. I wasn't sure but I got the feeling that she was trying to avoid the guy.

If she wanted me to chase her, then I would. She was so worth it.

When Diana re-emerged five minutes later, I was standing right there waiting for her. "What do I gotta do to get you to leave with me?"

"Kwon," she laughed nervously. "I don't turn tricks."

"That's good...'cuz I'm no trick. Look, I don't usually do this...but I want you. And I'm prepared to spend any amount of money to have you."

Over my shoulder, I saw the guy she was avoiding watching closely. There was obviously some unspoken tension between the two. I was sure that she was in an uncomfortable position. Stuck in the middle of who I presumed was her ex and me. The man who was marrying a dear friend of hers, and yet I was here, in her face, trying to make something happen.

"What about Roxie?" she asked. "Do you think she would like that?"

All of a sudden, her 'admirer' walked up and stuffed a hundred-dollar bill in her bra. "Excuse me. When you done, I need to see you," he said before walking off.

Diana looked flabbergasted. I chose to give her some space to sort out her thoughts. "Think about it," I said, heading back to my section. It was ultimately up to her to decide.

37

DIANA

Snatching the hundred-dollar bill out of my bra, I stomped over towards Rico. He was chilling at the bar, looking like he hadn't done anything wrong—except fuck up my hustle.

"Here! Take this fucking bullshit! I don't want your fucking money! I want you to leave me the fuck alone!" I had a visceral dislike for niggas who tried to drag me down and that's exactly what he was doing. Trying to pull me back into the underworld of sex trafficking.

"Aye, tone it down a notch, ma. I ain't come here for all that."

"You shouldn't have came here, period—"

"Why you so mothafucking resistant?" he asked with an attitude. "That's yo' mothafucking problem, man. You won't just follow my lead. When I go left you shouldn't be trying to go right. I need a submissive bitch."

"Nigga, you got a hundred submissive bitches."

"Yeah, but a real nigga need a *real* bitch. Not just a really submissive bitch."

I simply laughed at him and shook my head. "You know what, Rico? One day all your bitches gon' jump ship. What will you do then, huh? What will you do when the police eventually catch onto you? What's your plan B?"

"Having a plan B only distracts you from Plan A."

"Well, I don't wanna be apart of either plan. How 'bout that?"

Rico looked me dead in the eyes and said some shit I never expected to come out of his mouth. "I know about you and that nigga, Soul. I also know that he got a lil' girl..." An evil grin spread across his face. "And you know a bitch turns eighteen everyday."

I didn't like the fact that he was threatening Madison as a way of taunting me. She may've not been my child, but I would've cut his mothafucking balls off if he touched her. "...How the fuck you know about that?

"I know a lot of shit."

Hearing him say that made me wonder just how much he knew.

"End it," he said. "Before I end it for you."

38

KWON

When I got back to the section, Jisoo was looking at me with a confused expression on his face. He wanted to know what happened. I wanted to know the same.

"I thought you wanted that," he said.

I took a seat beside him. What I really wanted was every organ in her mothafucking body...but she seemed preoccupied with the asshole who'd interrupted us. All of a sudden, I noticed a pretty, tall fair-skinned woman with jet black hair. For the moment, she temporarily distracted me from Diana.

Nodding my head to Jisoo, I silently communicated my interest. He took off to retrieve her at the same time my business line started ringing. Realizing that it must've been important, I finally answered the call.

"This better be good."

"Well, I'm sorry to tell you this, but it isn't good at all. Something terrible has happened to your family."

***

"YOU TOLD ME THAT FUCKER WAS DEAD!" I knocked everything that was on my office desk to the floor. "How can a dead man do all this shit?!"

Half a day later, I returned to Korea to find my home in shambles and one of my sisters dead. Dae and Hae-Won were currently in the hospital but Hae-Won's injuries were a little less critical. Sadly, Sun didn't even make it out of the house alive. Fate couldn't have dealt a more terrible blow. In addition to Sun's death, I'd also lost two of my best men as well as Seung—my outcast sister forced into servitude.

Sara and Kim stood in my office gaping silently at me like two, stupid ass little kids being scolded. I'd given them simple, concise instructions and they couldn't even follow them. And then to make matters worse, they'd lied about following the instructions. Now I was paying for it with the loss of a loved one and several friends.

"So what you're telling me is he didn't die in the explosion. And as a result, my sister is dead instead of him...?" My voice was uncharacteristically calm.

"Sir, with all due respect, who would've thought someone would survive that explosion?" Kim asked.

I paused for a second. "...You're absolutely right," I said. Suddenly, and without warning, I ran towards him and stabbed him directly in the chest. "You're the cause of my sister suffering..." I twisted the knife, wanting him to feel every inch of my pain. "So now you must suffer."

Snatching the blade out of his chest, I watched as thick, dark red blood spurted everywhere. Kim immediately clutched his chest, his eyes wide open in horror. He staggered a bit before finally dropping to his knees. Grabbing him by his hair, I sliced his throat deep enough to sever his jugular.

After killing him, I tossed his body to the floor like a ragdoll.

Before Sara could say anything in her defense, I pulled my gun out and shot her in the head at point blank range.

POP!

I was tired of looking at their sorry asses. Neither one of them served me any purpose if they couldn't fulfill my simplest of requests.

My sister's shirt was covered in Sara's DNA. Gi was standing calmly in the corner of the room. She didn't bat an eyelash when the gun went off or when I savagely killed Kim. Like me, she'd grown accustomed to seeing death.

POP!

POP!

POP!

POP!

I filled each of their bodies with several more slugs until I finally ran out of ammo. Killing them actually made me feel a tiny bit better...but I wouldn't be fully satisfied until Magyc was in the ground.

"I need you to make funeral arrangements."

Gi looked confused. "For them or for Sun?"

"What do you fucking think?" I looked down at Kim and Sara's dead bodies. "Call the cleaners. Have 'em burn these bitches. They don't deserve a proper burial."

Grabbing my father's sword from above the mantle, I proceeded to clean it with my handkerchief. Everyone had a job to do and mine was to get retribution for the blood shed and the woman of mine who was missing. While I prepared to search for Roxie, I had Jisoo rounding up bodies in Atlanta for transport. The show still had to go on—even with the unfortunate news.

The money can't make itself.

And if you want something done right, you gotta do it yourself.

"Where are you going?!" Gi asked.

"To get my fucking fiancé back."

39

MAGYC

Roxie was madder than a mothafucka when I turned down her offer to help and sent her ass back home instead. She wanted to take down Kwon with me but I didn't want her in the middle. Even more, I didn't want her to get hurt.

This shit between me and Kwon wasn't a game, and I couldn't risk gambling with her or Rain's life. I wouldn't forgive myself if something happened to her. I already felt bad enough for letting her leave in the first place. When she told me that she was going out of the country with Kwon, I should've nipped that shit in the bud then—but I allowed my pride to get the best of me. I don't know what type of fuck shit I was on.

As much as it fucked me up, I watched her leave with a nigga that I knew wasn't shit. Now that I'd finally gotten her back, I wasn't going to let her go again. I'd almost lost her to Jag once and I'd be damned if I let some shit like that go down a second time. I'd die before I let a mothafucka hurt her or Rain. This was a war that I had started and had to finish—without her.

When Roxie told me where to find Kwon's warehouse, I thought about blowing his shit up but he had the whole place heavily secured for up to five miles surrounding the perimeter. No one—and I meant—no one was getting up in that mothafucka undetected. Not even the police, who Roxie explained was on his payroll.

Since it was hard to get to a man like Kwon on his own turf, I decided to go back to the states and wait for him to come to me. Roxie was pissed that I didn't let her stay with me, and her going back home was out of the question. Instead, I made her stay somewhere that was safe, out of the way, and guarded by people who I trusted and knew would protect her. I didn't want Kwon finding her...but if and when he did finally come looking for me, I'd be ready for his ass.

If he thought what I did to his family was fucked up, then he had no idea what I had in store for him. By the time I finished with that mothafucka, he was gonna regret ever fucking with me and mine's.

40
DIANA

The following Saturday, Soul surprised me with a beautiful date on the lake that wasn't just your average picnic. He went all out to make it unique and special, using an onshore boat to play "*Love Jones*" on the projection screen. Candles were lit all around, adding a majestic feel to the scenery.

Damn. I guess chivalry ain't dead...

It was by far one of the most charming things a man had ever done for me. And ironically, "*Love Jones*" just so happened to be my favorite movie. Neatly packaged in plastic containers were hearty helpings of curried chicken salad, succulent shrimp with vegetables, mojito watermelon, and, s'mores cookies.

"I can't believe you did all this? This is amazing, Soul. I—I'm at a loss for words...I mean...No one's ever done anything like this for me."

"Depending on how you act, I can show you much more."

***

After our picnic date, Soul took me to an African spot over on Buford Highway where he met his brother Quest and chopped it up for a minute. Wiz Kid's "*Show U D Money*" poured the subwoofers and everybody was dancing, drinking, and blowing on some gas. Quest and his boys had two sections in the corner of the club and enough bottles to share with everyone in the lounge if they chose to. It was one of his homies birthday and they were all celebrating.

Shortly after we arrived, several waitresses came out carrying bottles, sparklers and ice buckets. I assumed the bottles were for drinking but instead his niggas poured all of the expensive champagne on the birthday boy, completely soaking the cushions and floor in bubbly. I had never witnessed anything like it.

This was my first time in an African club and the entire vibe was different, mellow. Quest's camp welcomed me in with open arms and all of his friends were mad cool—even the females who were with them.

I was surprised when Soul introduced me to everyone as his girl. And even though we weren't on that level, I didn't correct him because honestly, I welcomed the idea of being his woman.

Buzzed off marijuana and Hennessey, I danced all night to Afrobeats. When DJ Maphorisa's "Soweto Baby" started playing Soul finally joined in too. Well...technically, he didn't dance. He simply stood behind me, gripping my waist, while smoking a cigarette. He allowed me to do all of the work, and for once, I didn't mind.

You must become my lady...

You drive me crazy...

Pushing it back up on him, I allowed the melodic lyrics to take over me. "Don't fucking play with me," Soul whispered in my ear. "'Cuz I'll punish your ass when we get back to the crib."

"Maybe that's what I want..."

***

When we finally got back to his place, I just knew that we were about to get intimate—but surprisingly we were both in for an unexpected twist. His daughter, Madison and her baby sitter were wide awake and waiting for us in the living room.

"What'chu doing up still, lil' lady? It's well past midnight," he noted, checking his Breitling to be sure. "Yo' ass should be in bed."

"I wanted to wait up for you..." she whined.

"Well, I'm back now, so off to bed you go."

"Daddy, who's that?" the 8-year old asked, blatantly ignoring his request.

Soul awkwardly introduced us and I couldn't help but wonder how many women his daughter had met. Secretly, I hoped that it wasn't something he did often because deep down inside I wanted to be special.

"Madison, this is my friend, Diana. Diana,

this is Madison."

Madison politely walked over to shake my hand and it was nice to see that she had manners. Nowadays, that seemed like such a rarity with these newer generation of kids.

"Hello, Madison. It's very nice to meet your acquaintance. Your father has told me so much about you."

"Well, he certainly hasn't mentioned you to *me*," the babysitter spoke up. She was a 60-something year old woman that reminded me of Cicely Tyson. "And she's pretty too. Where have you been hiding this one, Kwame?"

Kwame?

At least now I knew what his real name was.

Soul chuckled in amusement. "When the time was right, I was gonna introduce her to everyone."

"Well now's as good a time as any," she said, extending her hand. "My name's Greta...or Miss Orr...whichever you prefer."

"Pleased to meet you, Miss Orr." I was relieved that his family was both friendly and accepting of me.

"So has he told you about me? Or are we both out of the loop?"

Soul smiled and scratched his head, clearly put on the spot. "Greta practically raised me and Quest after coming over to the states as boys. She's like a mom to me."

Suddenly, Madison butted into the conversation. "Did that hurt?" she asked, pointing to the tattoos on my arms. Sometimes I forgot that the majority of my body was inked up.

"Yes...it did. But for me, it was worth it." Each of my tattoos were symbolic and meant something to me, even if no one else could relate.

"Daddy, when can I get a tattoo?" she asked Soul.

He pretended to think about it. "How' bout in 60 years or so."

"*Daaaddy!*" she whined.

"Nah, don't daddy me. Gon' get ready for bed."

Madison walked off, sulking all the way to her bedroom. Soul had her cute ass spoiled senselessly. She was a spitting replica of him down to the eyes. It didn't make any sense how adorable she was.

After bidding us farewell, Miss Orr departed, leaving me and Soul to the privacy we'd been longing for ever since we got back. We could've very well got it popping, but as soon as he took a seat on the couch he nodded off. And instead of waking him, I simply rested my head in his lap and fell asleep with him. Truth be told,

I couldn't have been any more at peace.

***

The following morning, I was awakened by the tantalizing scent of apple smoked bacon, French toast, eggs, and roasted potatoes. I had to go inside the kitchen just to make sure that it was actually Soul cooking and not some imposter. He was shirtless and barefoot with nothing but sweatpants on.

There were a few faint scars on his back that left me curious. *I wonder if those are tribal markings too.*

"Good morning," I greeted.

"Morning, beautiful. How'd you sleep?"

I smiled at him. "Better than I have in a while."

Soul smiled as well. This was my first time spending the night at his place. "Is that so?" he asked.

"Well...you know I'd gotten used to waking up in a cell everyday. It's refreshing to wake up somewhere I *want* to be."

Soul raised an eyebrow. "Oh, so you wanna be here, huh?"

"You know that I do. I told you you're what I want..."

"And I told you, to make that happen you gotta change ya profession," he said. "Are you working on that still?"

I stalled with my response because I hadn't put much thought into quitting my job. Stripping was all I knew and the money was so good and convenient. "Yeah...I'm working on it," I lied.

Soul gave me a doubtful look but carried on with what he was doing.

I then decided it was best to change the subject. "Anyway, lemme found out somebody know they way around the kitchen."

"Normally, I don't cook," he admitted. "But lately, you got me doing a lot of shit I normally wouldn't."

Walking up behind him, I wrapped my arms around his firm midsection. He didn't know it but he had a similar effect on me. Normally, I didn't do this shit. I didn't fall as fast as I was falling for him, but being with him felt so natural, so right.

"Where's Madison?" I asked him.

"In her room, watching TV. You should peek your head in and say hi."

"Okay. I'mma do that." Padding barefoot towards her bedroom, I found her right where he said I would.

Madison was on her plush princess canopy bed watching the Disney channel without a care in the world.

"Good morning, Madison," I greeted.

She looked up at me and smiled. "Good morning."

"Should I call you Madison or Maddie?"

"It doesn't matter. Either or. Usually everybody just calls me Maddie."

"Alright then. Maddie it is. So...what are you watching?"

"K.C. Undercover. It's my favorite show! I really like Zendaya."

I chuckled a little. "That's your girl, huh?"

"Yes! I love her *sooooo* much!" she sang joyously. She then paused for a second. "Do you love my daddy?"

Her question instantly caught me off guard. "Umm...well..."

Before I could answer, Soul called out that breakfast was ready.

After washing our hands, we all sat at the dining room table like one big happy family. I'd never been close to my own because most of them weren't shit or either on drugs. But being with Soul and Madison made me feel whole, complete. Almost like I belonged, even though I wasn't her mom and Soul wasn't my man. Regardless of the missing titles, a girl could get used to this.

After a scrumptious breakfast and light

conversation, I helped Soul clean the kitchen afterwards. I loved how when I cooked, he helped clean and when he cooked, I helped clean. Teamwork really did make the dream work.

As I was wiping the countertop off, I noticed a piece of opened mail lying out, addressed to a Mr. Kwame Asante. The age listed was five years younger than he'd told me. "Soul! You're only 25?!"

I held the piece of paper up as evidence to keep him from lying.

"Why you going through my shit?" he asked, snatching the letter out of my hand.

I didn't even read the contents of it because I was too distracted by him lying to me about his age. Back when we first met he told me he was 30.

"Why you lying to me?" I asked.

"It don't matter. You already in love," he joked. But I was dead ass serious.

"I don't like being lied to," I told him with a humorless expression on my face. I thought about how Wayne had lied about being married and how Rico had lied in order to set me up. I couldn't take another man lying to me.

When Soul saw how serious I was he became just as serious as well. "You're right. You don't deserve to be lied to. And it won't happen again. I can guarantee you that."

"Yeah, whatever, nigga. I see I'ma have to tame yo' ass," I teased.

My comment was enough to elicit laughter from him.

"How the fuck you gon' tame a beast?"

We laughed at that one together.

"So you were only sixteen when you had your daughter?"

"See, that right there is why I told you I was 30—"

"Soul, I'm not here to judge you. You met me in prison—*in prison*," I repeated.

"You absolutely right. I should've been real," he agreed. "From here on out, you can expect nothing but honesty from me. Brutal honesty," he emphasized.

"Nah, I don't want it if it's brutal," I giggled.

He slapped my ass hard and gave it a rough squeeze. "You finna get some brutal dick. Get'cho ass in the room."

I laughed before walking off to his bedroom. I'd been waiting for this moment like a kid waiting on Christmas.

Walking over to his king size bed, I prepared to undress. I was just about to pull my top off when I noticed that the bottom drawer to his nightstand was partially open.

Allowing my curiosity to get the better of me, I leaned down and opened it wider. A photo album was situated neatly inside. Pulling it out, I carefully opened it and thumbed through the pages. Inside were pictures of Soul and Quest playing football in their teenage years. There were also pictures of them as children in Ghana. I stopped to analyze a photo that I assumed was their parents. Their father was a dark skinned man with strong, stern features while their mom looked biracial and had green eyes. She was beautiful and I definitely saw some of Madison in her.

I smiled because I was finally getting a peek inside of his personal life, which he rarely if ever discussed.

I continued to flip the pages until I finally came across a picture of him and a pregnant teenage girl—

Suddenly, the photo album immediately dropped from my hands when I saw who she was.

41

DIANA

Oh my God! That's who the fuck his baby mama is? You gotta be mothafucking kidding me! I couldn't believe what I was seeing. Rico's bottom bitch Milena was Madison's mother. Now I understood why she'd abandoned her role as a mother. She would rather turn tricks for that fat ass nigga. The mere thought of them disgusted me.

Prior to my arrest, me and Milena had been real tight. We'd even fucked around occasionally...but when that bitch got up on the stand and lied on me, I lost all respect for her as a friend and as a woman.

I can't believe Milena is his baby mama.

Finding out the sad truth hurt more than anything. I had so many unanswered questions. Did Soul still deal with her from time to time? Did he and Rico know each other personally? Was there any bad blood between them?

I could only think the worse after finding out what I did. The shit was just too much to handle. I knew Atlanta was a small city but this was just ridiculous. Who would've known our pasts were somehow intertwined?

Rushing to put my clothes back on, I prepared to leave. I needed time alone to digest this new discovery because it had fucked me all the way up.

Soul was just about to walk in, when I brusquely walked past him.

"I have to go," I said, too ashamed to make eye contact.

Soul looked confused. "Why? Wassup?" he asked with genuine concern.

Just a minute ago everything was cool. Now I was practically running out of his place.

"I—I'm sorry. I really am but I gotta go."

Soul barely had time to react before I ran out of his crib on the verge of tears. Hopping inside my car, I started the engine and peeled off in a haste. I was so distraught by the news that I didn't notice that someone was following me.

42
MILENA

That night, Rico and I were at *Imperial Fez*, a popular Moroccan restaurant in the Buckhead area of Atlanta. There were belly dancers balancing fire on their heads and a plethora of interesting food dishes in front us— and yet he didn't look like he was having fun at all. Instead, it seemed like he had a lot on his mind, and I just knew he was thinking about that bitch Diana.

Ever since she'd left, he'd been acting differently. He no longer showered his girls with gifts and overwhelming attention. Instead, he neglected the fuck out of us, all because he'd lost the woman he was conditioning to be his main. And because I was his bottom, I felt some type of way about that shit.

In the beginning, before he even took off with this pimp shit, it used to be only us. I had met him at the tender age of seventeen and had been down for him ever since. There wasn't anything I wouldn't do for this nigga.

I sold my body for him, killed for him, hell, I even hit licks for him. I would probably die for him too if it came down to it. That was just how much I loved Rico. He was the love of my life, my father. My God. And as much as I cherished him, I no longer felt like I was getting the same amount of love in return. As a matter of fact, our relationship was starting to seem one-sided.

This bitch ass nigga really sweating this hoe.

I didn't think it was possible for a man like him to have his heart broken—and by a bitch that wasn't even relevant, in my opinion. Diana hadn't been around for nearly as long as some of us. I'd been rocking with him for almost ten years. Kina was going on eight, and Flo five. We were the ones truly loyal to him, the ones who'd take a bullet or catch a case if need be.

What the fuck is it about that hoe Diana that got him acting this way?

Rico was always saying '*What don't break a nigga, make a nigga*', but I couldn't tell. Apparently, he loved her far more than he'd let on and the shit was starting to make me feel jealous and vindictive. If I could, I'd throw acid in that bitch's face just to make sure he didn't go back to her.

I saw the way Rico had been chasing after her these last few weeks and I just wasn't feeling that shit. He had never chased me that way—not even after the times I'd threatened to leave and never come back. Usually, I did on my own anyway, but it was the principle that counted. And it fucked me up to know that Diana meant more to him than me.

"I did what you asked me to do

yesterday," I told him with an attitude. I was salty as fuck about him dragging me into him and Diana's drama, despite knowing how I felt about the situation. The bitch was gone and I wanted her to stay gone, but it was clear that Rico didn't want the same. He couldn't let her go, and he was willing to do any and everything in his power to get her back.

"Good shit," he said. "You sent it where I told you to?"

"Yes...I did," I answered gruffly.

"What the fuck is wrong wit'chu?" he asked, sensing my hostility.

"You really wanna know what the fuck is wrong with me?"

"I wouldn't have asked if I didn't."

"Well...I'll tell you what's wrong with me. You chasing after this bitch like she's done half the shit I've done for you!"

"*Chasing*? Nah, I ain't chasing no mothafucking body," he said defiantly. Rico was hot and bothered by my comment. Niggas hated being accused of what they were actually doing. "If anything, I'm making moves to have that bitch chase me!"

"Yeah, and you're using me to do it and that's fucked up!"

"Using *you*...or using Soul? Which one you more upset about?" he asked.

I immediately fell silent.

"It ain't even about that and you know it."

"Then what the fuck is it about then?"

"It's about us!" I cried. "What the fuck has she done for you? I mean really, please, tell me! I been with you from the jump! I gave up my life—my daughter to help put you in the position you're in! We started this shit together! We do everything together! We done fucked bitches together, niggas together—we done made millions together. Now that hoe comes along and you act like she's God's gift to the fucking world!"

"Now you talking too much—*and* you talking too mothafucking loud."

We were in a public setting and I was putting our business out there for everyone to hear but I didn't care. He needed to be reminded of my loyalty because I wasn't going to come second to any bitch.

"Mouth running like a fucking tab. You better close it now 'fore you end up with some more missing teeth."

The last time I'd talked this recklessly to him in public, he had knocked two of my teeth out and tore my ass lining out the frame. I couldn't sit down for an entire week and I had to get dental implants put in my mouth.

It was a huge price to pay for being too outspoken. Rico hated candidness.

"I'm not afraid of you," I said in Arabic.

"Well, apparently, I ain't whupped yo' ass enough. Don't think 'cuz I ain't fucked you up in a minute that I won't. I could give a fuck about these people around us. Don't test me."

Shaking my head, I decided that it was best to be quiet. The last thing I wanted was to be embarrassed in a public setting.

Why the fuck am I even here, I asked myself.

I was a former teenage beauty pageant contestant, with goals of one day being a super model. I had a beautiful daughter that didn't even know I existed. I had a promising future, even though I was a young mom—and now I was nothing but Rico's bottom bitch.

For the first time ever, I had to question my own sanity. I knew all the foul shit he did and was capable of and yet I stayed anyway.

Something's gotta fucking give.

A change needed to happen because I'd be damned if I competed for a nigga's heart. Especially a nigga who I'd proven myself to over and over again.

Rico won't realize my worth until I'm finally gone, I thought to myself. *And when I leave this time, I promise I'm not coming back.*

43
DIANA

For the last few days, I'd been ignoring all
of Soul's calls and text messages. I even stopped
coming in for work because I wanted to avoid
seeing him altogether. As much as it hurt me to
do him that way, I wasn't ready to face him yet.
Not after knowing what I now knew.

Since I hadn't been to work in a week, I
decided to go in that Saturday. If I was anyone
else, the manager would've hassled me about my
absence, but he didn't because I made him so
much money. My clients always bought the bar
out and every VIP section was sold well before
midnight. That was just how popular I had
become at Persuasion's. I was their cash cow so
he gave me certain special privileges—and
because of that the girls were always hating on
me.

As soon as I walked in the place, the
entire club was buzzing about how one of the
dancers was recently kidnapped while leaving
the club. A few of them had even quit out of fear
of being next.

I was sick to my mothafucking stomach
when I discovered that the victim was my girl,
Dynasty. Apparently, her body was found near
Lake Lanier. All of her major organs had been
removed. Hearing that fucked me up so bad that

I sat in the dressing room an hour just to let that shit marinate.

I just saw her ass a few days ago. I can't believe she's really gone.

Some people in this world were so sick that it was disgusting.

How could someone do that to Dynasty? She was such a sweet girl. She never bothered anyone. She came, made her money, and went home. She never gave any of the girls' problems. I just didn't understand why anyone would want to brutally murder her. It didn't make any sense to me.

After popping a Perc, I finally got my bearings and walked out of the dressing room. Much to my surprise, I spotted Soul standing near the bar with a scowl etched on his handsome face.

I thought about ignoring him but I knew that I couldn't avoid him forever. Swallowing my pride, I slowly made my way over towards him. He didn't look happy at all to see that I was right back in the strip club.

"You wanna tell me what that disappearing act was all about?" he asked.

"I'm afraid of what you'll think of me when I tell you..."

Soul's jaw tightened. "What'd you tell me the other day? I ain't here to judge you...All I want is for you to be real. 'Cuz I thought we were making good progress...but you skipped out on me...and didn't even have enough respect to tell me why."

Taking a deep breath, I prepared to tell him the truth...about everything. "I left because...I found out that Milena was your baby mama."

"You know Milena?"

"Quite well," I admitted. "We both were hustling for Rico."

Soul's left eye twitched at the mention of Rico's name—and that's when I knew that there was bad blood between them.

"Following his lead is how I ended up in prison in the first place..."

Soul looked disappointed to hear that. "Why the fuck would you follow that nigga? He don't know where the fuck he going." There was resentment in his tone when he said it, and I didn't blame him for feeling the way that he did.

"I agree. That's why I no longer am. I'm a shepherd not a sheep," I told him. "I'm done with that life."

"But you ain't done with *this*," he said, pointing to our surroundings. "You were given a second chance, and you're wasting it by doing the same shit you were doing before. You're better than this."

Hearing him say that brought tears to my eyes.

"What else am I supposed to do?" I asked him. "I have no degree. I have no work experience—and I'm an ex felon. How else am I supposed to take care of myself?"

Soul gently pulled me towards him. "You let me worry about that," he said.

"Soul—"

He quickly interrupted me. "Look, do you wanna build or do you wanna bullshit?"

44
SOUL

The following morning, I was instructed to meet the warden in his office. I had just clocked in when a fellow officer let me know that he wanted to see me. It wasn't often that he called me in so I wasn't quite sure what the meeting was in reference to. Nevertheless, I complied.

When I entered the warden's office, he was seated behind his desk with a somber expression on his face. There was a manila envelope in front of him. "Please...close the door behind you," he instructed.

I did as he asked before making my way over towards him.

"Do you know why you're here?" he asked.

"I don't."

Without another word, he opened the envelope and brandished a small stack of photos. Flipping through each one, he showed me every single picture, all the while shaking his head in shame.

The photos taken were of me and Diana—each one more provocative than the last. Someone had snapped pictures of us together in the strip club, when she was leaving my house, and when we were dancing at the African lounge.

It didn't take me long to realize that the nigga Rico was behind this shit. I wasn't a cat who had a lot of enemies so it wasn't hard to figure out that he was the one who furnished proof of my relationship with Diana.

This is what happens when fuck niggas have too much time on their hands.

"You were one of my best officers," the warden stated. "To say that I am disappointed is an understatement. You know that personal relationships with former inmates are strictly forbidden. We've had enough run-ins with the media on account of corruptness. I don't need those problems and neither do you."

I stood in front of his desk with my hands clasped together as I listened. He was the one who'd promoted me to chief officer and sadly, I had let him down.

"You've compromised me. You've compromised yourself...and you've compromised this prison," he said. "Unfortunately, I have to let you go..."

***

As soon as I left the prison for good, I headed straight to my brother's cigar bar. He had bought and used it as a front for tax purposes only. Other than the immediate people in his circle, nobody knew that Quest was a drug kingpin.

Before correcting my ways and going legit, I used to be about that life as well. But then I had Madison and she changed me for the better. But now that I was jobless, I had to come to my brother and humbly ask for a position in his operation. I had a daughter to take care of and bills to pay, and on top of that, I'd promised to look out for Diana. I couldn't do any of those things if I didn't have residual income.

When I pulled up to the spot, niggas were posted outside, monitoring who came in and who came out. It was supposed to be a public establishment, but not just anyone could walk in there.

Since I was family, they let me in with no problems. I found Quest in the lounge area, chilling with his right hand Ced. He was about 5"10, 5"11 and he had thick, nappy dreads and gold teeth.

There were a few ladies in there as well, but when he saw me walk up he dismissed them. Quest knew that I was there to talk about something important because I never showed up at his spot unannounced.

"I need to holla at'chu 'bout something," I said.

"Wus good?"

I looked over at Ced who was still sitting there. He was Quest's shooter and never ever left his side. Hell, I was his brother and he was still on guard.

"Aye, give us a minute, bruh."

"Aight."

Standing to his feet, Ced left the section, granting us some privacy. What I had to say was for my brother's ears only.

"Them pussy mothafuckas let me go."

"Damn. The prison? That's fucked up. You been with them niggas for over five years. Why the fuck they let you go?"

"'Cuz I started fucking around with this chick that used to be in there. And they can't let a mothafucka live their life. I mean, shit, she already done her time. What the fuck else do they want?"

"Damn, they tripping over that shit? That lil' shit?"

"It ain't shit though...'cuz a nigga gon' be aight regardless."

"Don't worry about it, bruh. You know I'm ten toes down in the game. We definitely gon' be aight."

Quest stood up and led me downstairs to where his vault was located. I thought he was about to give me some work but instead he handed me a duffel bag full of money. There had to be at least $50,000 inside.

"Nah, nah...I want in..." I said, turning his

money away.

Quest gave me a surprised look. "You *sure* you wanna do that?" he asked. "Nigga, you ain't been in the game a minute."

"Just know...I don't want no handouts."

45

MILENA

Since Rico's plan was to get Diana back, my plans were to get my family back together. After showering, I slid into a pink form-fitting maxi dress, and dabbed a little bit of Chanel No 5. on my neck and inner wrists. Lightly packing a few clothes, I grabbed some cash out of the safe and headed to the Miami International Airport.

Rico wasn't home at the time I'd left, so I didn't have to worry about him questioning me on where I was going. As far as I was concerned, my whereabouts were no longer his business.

The flight back home was less than two hours long, and as soon as I landed, I caught an Uber straight to Soul's crib. I had to do some digging to find his address, and I'd had it for a minute, but it wasn't until now that I decided to finally use it.

It was a quarter after 5 p.m. when I arrived at his place, and his Audi was parked in the driveway so I knew that he was home.

After tipping my driver, I climbed out and sashayed to the front door. I had to take a deep breath before knocking, because it had been eight long years since I saw him and Madison. Hell, my daughter didn't even know what I looked like.

Raising my fist, I tapped lightly on the surface and waited for him to answer. I felt nervous, anxious, and excited all in one breath. The only thing I could think about was reuniting with him and starting over because this shit with Rico was dead. It was finally time for me to let that lifestyle go.

After what felt like forever, Soul finally answered the door. For several seconds, we simply stared at one another in silence.

"What the fuck is you doing here?" he asked.

"Can I come inside so we can talk?"

Soul scratched his head. "Nah, I don't think that's a good idea."

"I caught a plane to talk to you? Now I can't come in?" I really just wanted him to let me in that bitch so I could seduce his ass. *He can front all he wants but he know he miss this pussy.*

"That sounds like a personal problem. That ain't got shit to do with me. Plus, I'm busy right now...So you gon' have to catch that plane back to where ever you came from."

"Really? That's how you gon' do the mother of your child?"

"Last time I checked, you wasn't a mother," he said. "Madison's almost nine years old. You ain't been around for none of her birthdays."

"Well...I'm here now...Don't that count for something?" I tried to reach out and touch him but he backed away. "Damn...so it's like that..." I was hurt. I don't know why I foolishly expected him to welcome me home with open arms.

"It's *just* like that..." he confirmed. "And you might wanna back up...'cuz I don't wanna smash ya fingers in the door—"

"So I can't see Maddie?"

"I don't want her seeing you like this. Coke hanging out the corner of ya fucking nose, higher than a giraffe's ass. What'chu need to see about is getting yo' mothafucking life together. We good over here."

I quickly wiped away the residue underneath my nose. I had done a line in the backseat of the car on the ride over, but it was only because I was nervous about seeing him. "Soul—"

"Go, Milena. Just go...Go right back to that nigga...I ain't got shit for you over here."

Suddenly, I burst into tears. "Soul, please—"

"I don't wanna hear it, Milena."

"Is everything okay?" I heard a woman ask in the background.

Her voice sounded strangely familiar.

"Diana?"

When she walked into view, I damn near lost it. I wanted to claw that bitch's mothafucking eyes out. "What the fuck is *she* doing here?!"

I didn't even give him a chance to respond before I ran up and started swinging.

46

MILENA

Soul roughly seized me from behind before I had the opportunity to hit her. "Man, what the fuck is you doing?! Is you fucking crazy?!"

"Really, Milena? *Really*? You gon' fucking swing on *me*?" Diana asked.

"Bitch, I'm sick of you, hoe! First Rico, now Soul?! Why don't you crawl back under the jail where you belong, bitch! I'm so mothafucking tired of yo' ass, hoe!"

All of a sudden, Madison stepped into the foyer to see what all the noise was about. "Daddy? Who is that?"

"Nobody! Go back to your room!" he demanded.

Diana quickly whisked her away so that she didn't see me kicking and hollering like I'd lost my mothafucking mind. *So he got this bitch raising my daughter too*, I thought. It fucked me up to hear him tell her that I was nobody. But sadly, it was my own fault that she didn't know who I was.

"Get the fuck outta here, man, with that bullshit!" he yelled, forcing me outside.

Angered and hyped up off my emotions, I stooped to an all time low by spitting in his face.

"Fuck you!"

Soul snatched me up by my throat so damn fast I thought he was going to snap my shit. "Did you just fucking spit on me—I COULD FUCKING KILL YOU, BITCH—"

"Soul! Don't!" Diana said, coming to my rescue. "It ain't worth it. Just let it go."

Listening to her words of wisdom, he finally released me and I anxiously sucked in oxygen. A few more seconds and I would've died from asphyxiation.

Secretly, that was just what I wanted...to die. Since Rico didn't love me anymore and Soul didn't want me back, I felt like I had nothing to live for. I couldn't sell pussy for the rest of my life. It just wasn't a way to live. The money meant nothing to me if I didn't have the love and support from those I cared about.

"You right," Soul agreed. "She ain't fucking worth it."

And with that said, he slammed the door in my fucking face. My weak attempt at gaining his love had failed miserably.

***

After the incident at Soul's, I went on a complete coke binge and got fucked up. Before I knew it, I was standing on the edge of the CNN building in downtown Atlanta, contemplating on ending it all. I thought about all of the wasted years I'd spent on a man who had never loved me. I felt so foolish, so motherfucking naïve.

How could I have allowed that sorry ass nigga to treat me this way for so long?

The question burned in my brain as I contemplated suicide. Every time that I blinked, I envisioned how my funeral would play out; the people who would attend, the fake ass tears that would be shed. Sad to say, I never imagined things would one day lead to this.

Gentle cricket noises could be heard in the distance, coupled with the sounds of impatient drivers beeping their horns. The full moon illuminated the dark, starry skies stretching overhead.

As my toes hung over the ledge, a strong gust of wind blew through my hair and an uneasy chill sat on my heart. I was barefoot in nothing but a Chanel cocktail dress and smeared makeup. A night of nonstop drinking and heavy drugs had me not giving a fuck about my appearance lately—which was totally unlike me. Normally, I was always on my shit, but because of him, I was now at an all-time low.

I can't believe I'm really at this point...

Blinded by emotions, I was too upset to realize that what I was preparing to do was the dumbest thing ever. Contrary to popular belief, I had always been a smart girl, with a fair amount of rationality and good judgment. But the day that I fell in love with him—the day that I gave my heart to that selfish, trifling ass bitch, all my common sense pretty much went out the window. For years, I had played the fool for a nigga who had been playing me the whole time.

I had done everything under the sun to prove my loyalty to a man that didn't even respect me. I'd sold my body for him, I'd lied for him, hell I'd even killed for him. I had literally sacrificed everything and everyone I knew and loved for him. I'd given him my all and in return he gave me shit. As a matter of fact, every man I ever loved gave me shit.

God, I feel so fucking stupid...

Warm tears cascaded down my cheeks as I took a small step forward. I shivered a bit at the rush of cool air that greeted me. The heels of my feet were now the only things keeping me grounded. One more inch and it'd all be over...

When I looked down, I saw heavy traffic and walking pedestrians who were completely oblivious to the woman above them preparing to jump. I had never been so close to death.

To tell the truth, in that moment, I felt free. Like the chains around my wrists and ankles had finally been unshackled. *If this is what I have to do to make the pain go away, then fuck it...* To me, it was worth it.

I had nothing or no one to live for. Rico wasn't fucking with me, Soul hated me, my daughter didn't even know who I was. It was no point in going on another day.

A crooked grin lingered in the corner of my lips. It was the first time I had smiled in ages, and for once, I felt like I was the one in control of my destiny. Like the weight of my burdens had finally been lifted. Closing my eyes, I prayed for atonement before leaping off the edge of the building...

46
SOUL

That Sunday, I decided to take Diana and Madison to church. I hadn't been in a while myself and with everything that had been going on lately, I felt like it would be good for all of us.

The unexpected visit from Milena really messed me up and threw me off. Not to mention the fact that I was back hustling now to make ends meet. It seemed like the devil was busier than ever.

There was once a time when I attended church regularly, but somewhere along the way, I'd fallen off. But when I woke up that morning, I realized there was no place I wanted to be more than in the Lord's house.

Dressed in our Sunday's best, we sat three rows from the pew and listened to the preacher deliver a powerful sermon that resonated with me.

"Jeremiah 29:11. For I know the plans I have for you, declares the Lord. Plans to prosper you and not to harm you. Plans to give you hope and a future."

***

After church, I took the girls to get some ice cream and then we all hung out at Chastain Park. It was a nice, sunny day and the weather was perfect so I thought why not? Normally, I was always busy and didn't have the time to take Maddie to the playground. But since I no longer had my second job, I had a bit more freedom.

I held back from telling Diana that I'd gotten fired because I didn't want her thinking that it was her fault—and I damn sure didn't tell her about me selling drugs now. I'd made my bed and now I had to lay in it.

I knew what the consequences were and I chose to take that risk and I didn't regret it at all. Even though we were moving at a rapid pace, I found myself falling for her more and more each day—and we hadn't even fucked yet.

It was refreshing getting to know each other without sex clouding our judgment. Usually, I wasn't one to show much restraint when it came to intimacy. But the fact that we were waiting only seemed to add more value to what we already had. And when we finally did decide to take that step, I knew that it would be special.

"Why you looking at me like that?" Diana asked with a smile. She stopped pushing Madison on the swing to come over and talk to me.

"Just thinking..." I said.

"'Bout what?"

"'Bout us...our future..."

"Oh, so you see us having a future, huh?"

"I see a lot of shit in store for us."

Diana's smile grew even wider. "Is that so?"

Before I could answer, Madison started calling my name. "Daddy! Daddy, look! I'm about to jump!" Pushing herself off the swing, she leapt to her feet like an acrobat. "Did you see it? Did you see it, daddy?"

"I saw it. Good job."

Madison resumed playing on the playground and I continued on with our conversation. Pulling Diana towards me, I held her close, savoring the sweet scent of her perfume. "I wanna take you and Maddie outta town, somewhere nice next weekend...Maybe Jamaica or Costa Rica."

"That sounds nice," she said." It also sounds like somebody must've just gotten a raise."

If only she knew...

I was just about to say something when I heard Madison's high-pitched screams, followed by a door slamming shut. Before I could recognize what was happening, the van that she was inside of skirted off.

I practically threw Diana to the ground as I took off running after the vehicle. "MADISON!"

My heart went into overdrive as I

watched the van bend the corner with my baby girl inside. *How the fuck could I have let this shit happen?*

"MADISON!"

Tears spilled from my eyes when I realized that she'd been kidnapped right from under my nose.

"*Madison*?!" My voice broke from emotion and heartache. I wanted to fucking die. This shit was not happening. It was not real. It couldn't be.

I stood there in denial for several second, mentally kicking myself. This had to be the worst day of my mothafucking life.

"*FUCK*!"

I screamed that shit so loudly that a nearby group of birds scattered in fear. I couldn't and wouldn't accept that she was gone. Was this shit really happening?

When I turned around, I saw Diana standing several feet away with an alarming look on her face. Suddenly, I ran up and wrapped my hands around her throat. "WAS IT HIM?!" I screamed through clenched teeth. "Was it that fuck nigga that took my baby girl?! ANSWER ME, BITCH!" I screamed, viciously shaking her.

Unfortunately, she couldn't because she was unable to breathe. I was strangling the life out of her but I didn't care. If she had anything to do with Maddie's disappearance, I would kill this bitch with my bare hands.

Diana tried to answer but her windpipe was crushed. I watched as her face swelled and turned beet red. She clawed at my hands desperately, but it only made me squeeze tighter.

"*Was it him*?!"

Diana's eyes rolled into the back of her head...and it wasn't until then that I realized I'd lifted her off of her feet.

She was damn near on the verge of passing out when I finally let her go.

Diana dropped to the floor, gasping for air. She tried to speak but her voice came out hoarse.

I didn't have time for her bullshit. Racing to my car, I hopped inside and started the engine, ignoring Diana as she called out my name. Nothing was more important to me than getting Madison back.

47
MAGYC

Me, Roxie, and Rain were in a jeep with two of my homeboys as I transported her to a vacation home that Jude owned in the outskirts of the city. I was constantly moving her around to throw Kwon off in case he was trailing us.

Until that mothafucka was dead, I had to do everything in my power to protect her and Rain. Roxie hated that she couldn't live in one place and be happy. Even more, she hated that we couldn't be together, but I couldn't risk putting her life in jeopardy. I'd risk my own before I allowed anything to happen to her.

"How long are we gonna do this, Magyc?" she asked.

"Until this shit is over…"

"And when will it be over?" she pressed. "When will it end, because this just ain't no way to live. It isn't healthy for me and it isn't healthy for Rain."

Massaging my temple, I sighed in frustration. "I'm trying to do everything I can," I told her. "All I wanna do is keep you two safe. You may not like the way I'm going about it but it's the best I can do for right now."

Roxie released a deep breath, folded her arms, and looked out of the window. I could tell there was a lot she wanted to say but she held back from doing so. She could be as angry as she wanted with me, but at the end of the day, I was only trying to protect her.

Reaching over, I placed my hand on top of hers and massaged her knuckles. Hopefully, we wouldn't have to do this for much longer. The sooner I handled that nigga Kwon, the sooner we could get back to our lives without disruption.

"You still love me?" I asked her.

Roxie smiled weakly. "You know that I do..."

Before I could say anything else, a truck slammed hard as fuck into us, causing the jeep to flip over.

48

DIANA

There was so much shit on my mind when I walked through the door of my apartment. My heart was heavy. Witnessing Madison get kidnapped before my very eyes really fucked me up. And while I didn't want to believe that Rico was capable of that, he was the only person I could think of who would do such a thing. After all, he'd clearly threatened her at the club the last time we saw each other.

Pulling out my cellphone, I took a seat on my couch and checked to see if I had any missed calls. I wasn't surprised that Soul hadn't reached out, and I could only hope that he didn't do anything stupid in retaliation that might land him in trouble—or worse, dead.

I can't believe this shit.

Staring at the wallpaper of my iPhone, I contemplated calling 911 and telling them everything about Rico. Normally, I didn't agree with snitching, but if he had anything to do with Madison's kidnapping, then he deserved to rot in a fucking jail cell.

I had just pressed the number 9 on my keypad when I suddenly heard the sound of a gun clicking behind me. Turning around in my seat, I noticed Yuri's sister, Tabitha standing there with a loaded pistol in her hands.

My stomach instantly dropped into the pit of my stomach. The last time we'd saw each other was when her son was hit and killed in the parking lot of a Cleveland mall. It was because of me she was even there to begin with.

If I hadn't been screwing her husband Wayne, he and their son would still be alive. The guilt of what I'd done was what caused me to move to Atlanta. I was supposed to be starting over...but sadly my demons had finally caught up with me.

"You look surprised to see me," Tabitha said. Her gun was aimed steady in my direction. She laughed a little. "Did you really think I would spare you?" In her eyes, I saw insanity. A loving mother and wife had been turned into a psychotic, vengeful maniac—and it was all my fault.

"Tabitha..." I slowly stood to my feet. Her gun followed my every movement. "You don't have to do this..."

"The hell I don't!" she said. "You took my son away from me! Now I have to take your life!"

"Tabitha—"

POP!

A single bullet tore clean through my leg, causing me to fall to the floor, howling in pain. I couldn't believe this crazy ass bitch had really shot me. Suddenly, it dawned on me that I was going to die today. All because of one mistake I had made in the past.

Tabitha smiled at the sight of me in agony. Almost like she enjoyed seeing me suffer. Slowly making her way over towards me, she kept her pistol aimed at me. "You have no idea how many times I dreamed about this moment," she said. "How many nights its kept me awake—"

"Tabitha, please!" I cried. "You don't have to do this!"

"You don't get it, do you?" she asked. "I *have* to do this...It's the only thing that'll offer me peace...'Cuz trust me, you have no idea what it's like to lose a child..."

"Tabitha, I'm begging you—"

"If I were you, I'd save my words for my final prayers..." She then waited for a moment. "Oh...you don't have any?" She shook her head and scoffed. "Can't say I'm too surprised a woman like you lacks faith. You had no remorse for fucking a married man! You had no sympathy for killing my son!" she screamed. "I may as well do humanity a favor and put you out of your misery. The last thing I'd want is another family to suffer at your hands."

Tears rose to my eyes when I thought about Madison and Soul. Maybe Tabitha was right. Maybe I was better off dead. I'd caused more than enough pain and misery to last a lifetime. Maybe her killing me was for the best. Closing my eyes, I accepted my end. I was done begging, done asking for forgiveness.

The very last thing I saw was Tabitha pointing her gun at my head.

POP!

EPILOGUE

Madison trembled uncontrollably as she sat in the backseat of a van in the middle of two Korean men. They were the same men who'd been kidnapped her from the park when Soul and Diana weren't paying attention.

Madison was terrified and unsure of her fate. One minute she was playing in the park without a care in the world and the next she was being seized by foreign organ traffickers.

"I want my daddy!" she cried.

Everyone in the vehicle ignored her as she sobbed uncontrollably. She'd never been more afraid in her life. Suddenly, she scolded herself for wandering too far from the playground. She had only walked off for a second when someone hopped out and grabbed her. Before she knew it, she was inside a van with several strangers speaking a funny language.

Madison didn't know what was going on or why she was there. All she knew was that she was in trouble. "I want my daddy—"

Without warning, the man next to her slapped her hard in the face.

Initially, she was shocked after the assault. No one had ever hit her before, not even her father. Madison had been spoiled all of her life and she didn't know what it felt like to be physically punished.

Realizing that she was in a dangerous predicament, she started bawling in the backseat. She missed her father, she even missed Diana. She would've given anything to go back.

After hearing Madison's soft cries, Jisoo turned around in the passenger seat and looked at her. With a wicked grin, he said, "Don't worry little girl...It'll all be over soon..."

ABOUT THE AUTHOR

Jade Jones discovered her passion for creative writing in elementary school. Born in 1989, she began writing short stories and poetry as an outlet. Later on, as a teen, she led a troubled life which later resulted in her becoming a ward of the court. Jade fell in love with the art and used storytelling as a means of venting during her tumultuous times.

Aging out of the system two years later, she was thrust into the dismal world of homelessness. Desperate, and with limited income, Jade began dancing full time at the tender age of eighteen. It wasn't until Fall of 2008 when she finally caught her break after being accepted into Cleveland State University. There, Jade lived on campus and majored in Film and Television. Now, six years later, she flourishes from her childhood dream of becoming a bestselling author. Since then she has written the best-selling "Cameron" series and the highly-rated "Torn Between a Goon and a Gangsta" trilogy.

Quite suitably, she uses her life's experiences to create captivating characters and story lines. Jade currently resides in Atlanta, Georgia. With no children, she spends her leisure shopping and traveling. She says that seeing new faces, meeting new people, and experiencing diverse cultures fuels her creativity. The stories are generated in her heart, the craft is practiced in her mind, and she expresses her passion through ink.

To learn more, visit
www.jadedpublications.com

EXCERPT FROM "*I FELL IN LOVE WITH A REAL STREET NIGGA*"

1

KHARI

PRESENT DAY

With my 7-year old son Ali in tow, I carefully made my way to the visits hall where my fiancé awaited our arrival. This was only Ali's third time visiting his father in prison, because I hated him having to see his dad locked up. Normally, I didn't bring him with me to visitation but Aubrey insisted. He claimed his family was the only thing keeping him sane behind prison walls, so I refused to rob him of the privilege of being a father to his only child.

When me and Ali entered the somewhat noisy hall, we found Aubrey sitting alone at an empty stainless steel table, surrounded by fellow inmates and their chatty relatives. My smile widened as I approached him and he graciously returned it. He had a fresh cut and his face was groomed. It was nice to see that he was taking care of himself. I couldn't front. Even for a convicted felon, Aubrey looked good.

At 35, he was ten years older than me, dark chocolate, and somewhat rough around the edges. He had big, brown eyes, long lashes, and thick, juicy lips. There was a small scar along his jaw and one that ran through his left eyebrow that he told me was from a bar fight years ago.

Flaws aside, Aubrey was devilishly handsome. Slim, tall, and toned in build, he reminded me of an NBA player in his prime. Aubrey had always been a gym rat and he made sure it showed in his physique.

Covering over 60% of his body was a collage of decorative tattoos. The only areas that weren't tatted was his face and neck. His favorite one of all was the portrait of Ali on his upper arm. Our son was his proudest accomplishment.

Aubrey quickly stood to his feet to greet us. "*Waa gwaan, empress*," he said in a thick Caribbean accent. He was born and raised in St. Thomas and relocated to the U.S. ten years ago. "It's been a minute since I seen ya'll." Pulling me and Ali towards him, Aubrey hugged us tightly. It'd been almost four months to be exact, and although I wanted to see him more, work and school simply wouldn't permit it. Taking time off for the 3 ½ hour drive from Atlanta to Savannah was easier said than done.

"I tried to get out here last week but my schedule was hectic—"

"Guess what? You here though. That's all that matters. Not to mention, I had to prepare myself mentally before we linked up."

I could respect that he wanted to have his

mind right before he dealt with me. We all took our respectful seats, with Ali sitting closest to Aubrey. He was unashamedly a daddy's boy since Aubrey spoiled him. Ali gave a snaggle-tooth grin after his father playfully ruffled his short, curly hair. He had my hazel eyes, coffee complexion, and dimpled chin. Everyone said that he was a spitting image of me.

"So...how are you holding up?" I asked. It was nearly two years since Aubrey was arrested on drug and weapon charges. This was his third strike, so the judge and jury didn't cut him any slack at trial. I almost fainted in court when they read his sentencing. Ever since he'd left, my life just hadn't been the same.

"Same shit, different day."

Ali excitedly communicated through hand gestures. He was born with congenital hearing loss due to pregnancy complications. Aubrey never wanted Ali to feel different from other children so he overindulged when it came to spoiling him. Our son had all of the latest high tech gadgets, game consoles, and every special edition shoe known to man. Aubrey cherished his son and spared no expense when it came to him. He was a damn good father, which was why I'd stayed with him for as long as I did, in spite of his constant infidelities.

Prior to his imprisonment, Aubrey had a real problem with keeping his dick in his pants. As a well-known music producer and party host, he was always surrounded by aspiring models, artists, and thirsty hoes looking for a quick come up. There were some side chicks out there willing to do anything for the limelight. It wasn't until I threatened to leave him for good that Aubrey finally straightened up his act and proposed to me.

"Ali just said he misses you a lot." Since Aubrey was always in the streets or at the studio, he never bothered to learn sign language. Luckily for him, Ali was an expert when it came to reading lips. "Sometimes he wakes up thinking that you're still there," I told him. "Sometimes I do too…"

"You know you gotta nigga deep in his feelings about ya'll," Aubrey said. Pulling his son close, he kissed the top of his head.

It was a few weeks until Christmas and I hated that he wouldn't be home for the holidays. I could tell he was saddened that he couldn't physically be there for us.

"Have you heard anything from the lawyer?" I asked, changing the subject. We'd been working on an appeal ever since his conviction.

Aubrey scoffed and rolled his eyes. He hated whenever I brought up legal matters during visitation. "Nah…but don't trouble yaself about it, y' hear? A real nigga gon' stand where a real nigga land. As long as my family's good I ain't gon' ever lose sleep."

"Aubrey, by the time you get out your son will practically be an adult," I reminded him. "How could you sleep peacefully knowing that you'll miss out on him growing up?"

"You said the key thing...when I get out. You know they can't keep a real nigga down for long. I'mma still be there for him no matter what."

"How can you be there for him when you're in here?!" I yelled.

With a concerned expression, Ali asked if I were okay. He wasn't accustomed to seeing me lose my cool, and I prided myself on my patience. Simmering down a bit before I caused a scene, I raked a hand through my naturally curly hair and sighed. I hated for my son to see me worked up but our current state of affairs was ultimately taking its toll on me. Aubrey had been gone for over a year and I still wasn't used to his absence. Forcing a smile, I told Ali that I was fine in sign language.

He had no idea that it was a lie.

In fact, I was gradually falling apart. I never anticipated on raising our child alone. Because I had grown up in a two parent household, I wanted the same for our son. And as thankful as I was for the lifestyle Aubrey gave us, I would've chosen him over it any day.

Sensing my frustrations, he reached over and placed his hand over mine. The simple gesture alone made me relax a little. Aubrey had a knack for making me feel secure.

I met Aubrey while waitressing part-time at a family owned diner. I'd just started my freshman year in college and needed the extra money for books. He and his brother visited one day during lunch hours. They'd only been living in the states for three months at the time of our introduction.

Truthfully, I didn't immediately find Aubrey attractive. He was scruffy looking, overly confident, and a tad bit aggressive. But over time, I grew to love everything about him. He helped mold me into the woman I was today. He taught me a lot, and he was the first and only man I'd ever truly loved. With that being said, I eventually got over the crush I had on Cue. He moved to New York just before I went off to school and I never saw him again.

"I'm locked up, but my money ain't. You think these bars gon' stop a nigga from getting money? These bars ain't stopping shit. If anything, these bars taught me how to network better," he explained. "Can't shit stop me from taking care of my family."

There was a long period of silence between us before he spoke again.

"You still be in the church every Sunday?" Aubrey asked.

I'd been attending the Sunday services at

our local church devotedly. I even helped organize some of the special events. "Yes," I answered. "Every week."

"Aight, then have faith that shit's gon' get greater later."

Something about his words gave me hope. And he was right. He really did do everything he could to take care of his family. He may've been imprisoned, but his revenue consistently poured in like he was still in the streets.

Aubrey ran a lucrative drug business outside of his music career. He even he had a few loyal customers that were in the industry. Every month, he received packages that were shipped to different people's houses, and the niggas on his payroll sold the work on the streets.

Aubrey never had that shit around us; he never even had a shipment delivered to our house. He didn't want us exposed to his lifestyle, and I was fine with that because I'd never condoned him selling drugs in the first place. Since it was our main source of income I couldn't quite complain either. After all, it was the same money that funded my education.

Mama would've been so disappointed if she ever found out the truth about Aubrey. I had told her that he was arrested for failing to pay taxes. She didn't know about his life as a dealer. For years she'd been under the impression that he was nothing more than a music producer. Mama would've shunned me if she knew I'd fallen in love with a criminal.

As much as I wanted to confide in her, I knew that I couldn't. Mama already wasn't too fond Aubrey because of the issues I'd spoken to her about in the past. I mean, how could she respect a man who constantly lied, cheated, and abused her daughter?

Mama told me time and time again to leave him alone but I just couldn't. Honestly, this street shit and Aubrey's thugged out mentality turned me on. He made me feel important, like I was that bitch. Not to mention, he laid it down like a beast in the bedroom. He had me so gone that I didn't want to return. He had me sprung like a box mattress. Everything about him captivated me.

Aubrey was street, but he was also wise, patient, and clever. Being with him was like a breath of fresh air. Because he was older, he was a lot more mature than the young fuck boys I used to entertain. He'd gotten me at a young age and groomed me into the woman and mother I was today.

Shaking off those worrisome feelings, I caressed his hand and smiled. "I'll try to have faith..." It was the best I could come up with.

Aubrey sensed my uncertainty. "You can't try to have faith. You gotta *believe*," he stressed.

After several minutes of small talk and reminiscing, a C.O. finally notified everyone that visiting hours were over. Ali sulked and pouted since we had to leave, but I reminded him that we'd be back next month.

When Aubrey pulled me in for a firm, farewell hug, he whispered in my ear, "Make sure you keep things in line. We don't need you falling off track."

I knew exactly what he meant by that. "Aubrey, I'm too busy working and raising your son to be out here entertaining other men."

"That's real, stay focused," he said. "Do you think you can do me a favor though? You think you can cover my shit up next time you come here...'fore I have to *kill* one of these niggas." Out of nowhere, Aubrey snapped on one of his fellow inmates. "*Wah di bumboclaat wrang wid yu*!?" I assumed the man was from the islands as well since he'd started speaking broken English. The older man had been checking me out ever since I walked in.

"How 'bout I just wear a black trash bag instead," I said sarcastically.

Aubrey squeezed my ass and pulled me towards him. "Alright now," he said as if he were warning me. "*Mmm*." He gave my butt another firm squeeze and Ali quickly covered his eyes. He never cared to see our affection. "Dat mufucka back there gettin' fat," he teased. "I'mma have to make a way to get up in that. So the next time you come make sure you don't have no panties on."

With a flirtatious grin, I told him, "How about we just focus on one thing at a time."

Thankfully, my chubbiness transitioned into a curvy and voluptuous shape. I rocked a size sixteen with pride, but the extra weight was in all the right places. Everyone said that I had Ali to thank for that.

"Alright, queen." Aubrey kissed my forehead. Tilting my chin up to meet his gaze, he stared lovingly into my eyes. "I don't wanna have to wait long to see that pretty smile again."

"I promise you won't."

Aubrey ruffled his son's hair again before giving him a final hug. After saying our goodbyes, we parted ways.

"Bless up yaself," Aubrey called after me.

Right about now, I needed all of the blessings I could get if I planned on holding him down for this ten-year stretch. Looking down at my son, I suddenly had doubts about marrying a man in prison.

Would things get better? Would things get worse?

I had no idea how to cope with this shit and I wasn't sure where my life was going. Not to mention, I had a child to think about. It wasn't fair for me to drag him through this shit. Men could make things sound really good at rehearsal, but the outcome could be entirely different.

All of a sudden, I began to have doubts about everything in general. It was the first time since Aubrey's conviction that I actually questioned myself as well as my moralities.

2
KYLIE

I got broads in Atlanta...

Twisting dope, lean, and the Fanta...

Credit cards and scammers...

Hitting off licks in the bando...

Black X6, Phantom...

White X6 looks like a panda...

Going out like I'm Montana...

Hundred killers, hundred hammers...

My best friend Paige multi-tasked between twerking and smoking a blunt to Desiigner's *Panda*. She was a cute, slender Puerto-Rican girl, originally from the Flatbush area of Brooklyn, New York.

Paige was my partner in crime. We'd met in jail a couple years back and were both there for petty theft. Everyone—including my sister—thought she was a bad influence but I didn't give a fuck. I was a grown ass woman, free to make my own choice in friends.

Just then, Paige took off her leggings to watch her booty jiggle and shake in the full length mirror. Her pink Hello Kitty draws were riding insanely high up her ass while she danced but she obviously thought that shit was cute.

Paige was a ho, who'd seen more cocks than the walls of a sperm bank.

Thankfully, my bedroom door was closed. I knew how much the trap music and smell of weed bothered mama. Also, she wasn't particularly fond of Paige. She and Khari loved pretending they were holier than thou. They never liked my men, friends, or lifestyle. Oh well, fuck 'em.

At 25, I was still living at home. After losing the baby at 7 months, I just gave up on most shit in life, including independence. Khari went on to get a degree and have a kid while I pretty much stayed stagnant. The miscarriage had fucked me all the way up. I'd even started popping Percocet and stealing again just to fill the void inside of me. No one was happier than me about the pregnancy...and when my son died, I just lost it. I lost myself.

"What do you think about me getting ass shots?" Paige asked, interrupting my thoughts.

"Hoe, I'm thinking about that yeast infection you finna be stuck with. Anyway, we need to be focused on *making* money instead of spending it," I reminded her. "Speaking of which, how much you think we can get for all this shit?"

Laid across my mattress was all of the designer purses, expensive perfumes, and clothes we'd stolen from Nordstrom's a few hours earlier. Boosting had become my way of life.

Paige took a final puff on the blunt before passing it to me. "Hmm..." She looked over every item carefully while doing the math in her head. "Roughly, I'd say...close to a grand."

I sighed exasperatedly. "*Ugh!* That's it?! Bitch, I need a lick! Not this chump change we been making. I'm tired of Uber and riding the fucking bus. I need a car, bitch." The days of borrowing money from mama were over since I'd burned my bridges there. I had to make sure I was able to support me by any means necessary.

Paige placed a finger on her chin like she was thinking. "If we try to upsell—"

"*Upsell*?! Bitch, ain't nobody 'bout to spend big money on some yoga pants and Michael Kors bags. See, I told ya ass we should've hit one of them luxury stores like Gucci or Celine. But noooo, you ain't want to—"

"Dummy, that shit be secured as fuck. Plus, they got cameras like a mothafucka—"

"Lock-picking is my forte...and fuck a camera. I'll wear a hoodie or something," I argued. "Them bitches be running a couple grand easy. We could rack up a few thousands apiece with no sweat if we snagged a few."

"I don't know," Paige said, doubtfully. "Shit, I'm all for making a come up, but ain't nobody trying to go to jail. Hell, I just *got off* probation."

"Hoe, ain't *nobody* going to jail."

"Well, I say you go for it and let me know how that works out."

I rolled my eyes at Paige and shook my head. Sometimes she could be such a pussy. "You real crusty for that shit."

She opened her mouth to say something but was interrupted by the doorbell ringing. I almost expected mama to answer until I remembered that she and her boyfriend, Lenny were on a three-day cruise in the Bahamas. "All I'm asking is for you to think about it. Okay?" I said on my way out the room.

Padding barefoot to the front door, I stood on my tiptoes and looked through the peephole. Much to my surprise, there was no one standing on the other end. "What the hell?"

Chalking it up to some bad ass kids in the 'hood, I turned and walked away—

Ding dong.

Growling in frustration, I stomped back to the front of the house. When I looked through the peephole again there was still no one there. Fed up with the bullshit, I swung the door open in anger. "Look, whoever the fuck is playing on my gotdamn—"

All of a sudden, someone reached out and grabbed me.

3

KYLIE

A calloused hand clamped tightly over my mouth before I could scream for help. As I struggled in my captor's embrace, I felt his erection pressing into the small of my back. *Oh my God, this nigga about to rape me!* My throat stung as I desperately tried to call Paige's name. It was useless since my mouth was covered.

When I recognized who was holding me I finally calmed down. "Jamaal! You fucking asshole!" Never in a million years did I expect to see my ex. Then again, he had a habit of coming out the cut like Cosby victims.

Whap!

I hit him as hard as I could in the chest as he laughed hysterically like seeing me scared was the funniest shit on earth.

"It's not funny, Jamaal! You childish as fuck!"

Whap!

I hit him again, this time across his face. In one fluid motion, he grabbed my wrist and snatched me so close to him that our bodies were pressed together.

"That rough shit only makes my dick hard."

Disgusted by his words and mere presence, I pushed him away. "Boy, I wouldn't fuck you or any nigga that resembles you. And why the hell do you play so much? You almost gave me a damn heart attack! What is wrong with you? I seriously could've hurt you—"

"Man, hold that noise and gimme that tongue to suck on."

Jamaal leaned in to kiss me but I quickly moved away. "*Hell naw*! I don't know where the fuck your tongue been. Besides, it ain't even that type of party no more, Mall. It's been years since I last saw you. You always in and out. You can't just pop the fuck up whenever you feel like it and expect to get some mothafucking ass."

"Aww, girl, cut the games. You know you miss it."

"Nah, nigga. Run me that mothafucking money you owe me. That's what I'm missing."

Jamaal chuckled, clearly amused by my feistiness. He always told me my mouth was too smart for a soft nigga. "You real funny, you know that shit." He smiled, revealing his deep set of dimples. I always told him he reminded me of Juelz Santana but with dreads. Jamaal wasn't shit half the time, but the man was unquestionably fine. He was also trouble.

Eyeing the fresh fit and jewelry he had on, I quickly realized that he wasn't the same broke nigga I fell in love with. Everything was designer from the Versace shades perched on top of his head to the matching sneakers on his feet.

"You standing here looking like new money and shit, where my mothafucking cut at?" I asked.

"Man, calm down with all that shit, girl. Why you think I'm here?" Jamaal pulled off his Louis Vuitton backpack and handed it to me. "Real niggas do real shit."

After unzipping the bag, I eagerly peeked inside. Gasping in shock, I covered my mouth and looked up at Jamaal. There was a shitload of money in the backpack, each stack bundled tightly and labeled $10,000. If I had to guess, I'd say there was at least half a million present and accounted for.

"Damn, Jamaal. Where the hell did you get this kind of cash?"

"The details ain't important."

"Jamaal, I—are you for real? Boy, do not fucking play with me!" He only owed me $2,000 but I would've gladly taken all the money if he really was giving it to me. "I can have all of this? Are you serious? Are you fucking serious?"

"Dead ass."

"Jamaal...Oh my God! This is fucking incredible! Thank you! Thank you! Thank you God knows I really need this money! Oh my God!" Snatching out a single stack, I made it rain on my gotdamn self.

"Wait a minute, bitch...I'mma need you to calm the fuck down. Now there *is* one catch."

I sucked my teeth and blew out air. "Oh, boy, here we go." My mama said if something seemed too good to be true it probably was. "There's always a fucking catch when it comes to you. Well then...what is it?"

"Looks can be deceiving."

"What do you mean by that?"

"It looks real...but it's counterfeit."

"WHAT! Are you fucking serious? Boy, get the fuck outta here. What type of fool do you take me for?" Tossing the bag at his feet, I prepared to slam the door right in his damn face.

"Hol' up, hol' up...before you get so judgmental about it, I'mma need you to hear me out first." Jamaal quickly grabbed my elbow and turned me around.

"What else is there to say, Jamaal? You brought this fake ass money here thinking you was gon' get back in my good graces. I don't know who's stupider. You or me for believing you were really finna give me half a mil."

"But I guarantee every bill in that mufucka passes for the real thing," he said. "Go head. Pull out a band, thumb through it. You won't find a single defect. I put that on blood."

"And I'm supposed to believe that?"

"Look at it. Shit, that's all you gotta do."

Sighing deeply, I reached down, grabbed a stack of money from the bag, and looked closely at it. As sure as shit, it had the official blue band across every hundred. There wasn't a single imperfection in sight. The bills were absolutely flawless.

"You sure it'll pass for real?" I asked.

"Take that shit to the bank. You'll see."

"How could you be so sure? Have you tried to spend any of this money?"

"Go outside and look in the driveway."

Parked in front of the house was a brand new pearl white BMW convertible. It had a peanut butter wood grain interior, a fresh wax job, and custom Forgiatos rims that were at least six grand a piece. On the top of the hood was a huge, red bow.

"Fresh off the lot," he bragged. "The best for the best."

I hadn't even noticed the car until he pointed it out. "Oh, my God, Jamaal! You gotta be fucking kidding me! OH MY GOD! You bought me a car?!" I shouted with enthusiasm. "Hell yeah!" I was in complete shock and disbelief. I couldn't wait to floss and show out in my new car.

"Think of it as a peace offering." Jamaal pulled my face towards him. "Look, I know you think a nigga be on some bullshit. But now I got some shit that's gon' make everything right."

I wanted to believe he was being sincere, but the nigga had good ass penitentiary game. Jamaal was a habitual liar and a womanizer, who constantly sold dreams. "Jamaal...you know it's hard for me to trust you. You talking all this big shit now but you good for going MIA. Don't build me up just to tear me down—"

"Nah, we all the way to the top from here on out. No ceilings, baby. Enough of the games, a nigga tryin' to be on some real shit wit'chu."

"Yeah, I bet you are now that it's convenient for you. How do I know you ain't gon' be on that bullshit again?"

"Gimme a chance to prove it to you."

Because I felt myself getting emotional I quickly changed the topic. I hated for anyone—especially a man—to see me vulnerable. "Is this shit like...for real official? I mean like...*for real* for real? I won't run into any trouble spending this money, right? There won't be any problems?" I was still on probation so I had to tread very carefully.

"That money gon' spend itself."

"So I'm good?"

"You're great," Jamaal assured me. "Now can I get some of that mufuckin' tongue?"

"Nigga please. You ain't out the mothafucking doghouse yet."

"You still petty as fuck I see."

"Nah, I'm *real* as fuck."

VISIT AMAZON.COM TO GET YOUR COPY!

Made in the USA
Middletown, DE
30 December 2016